Five Magic Rooms

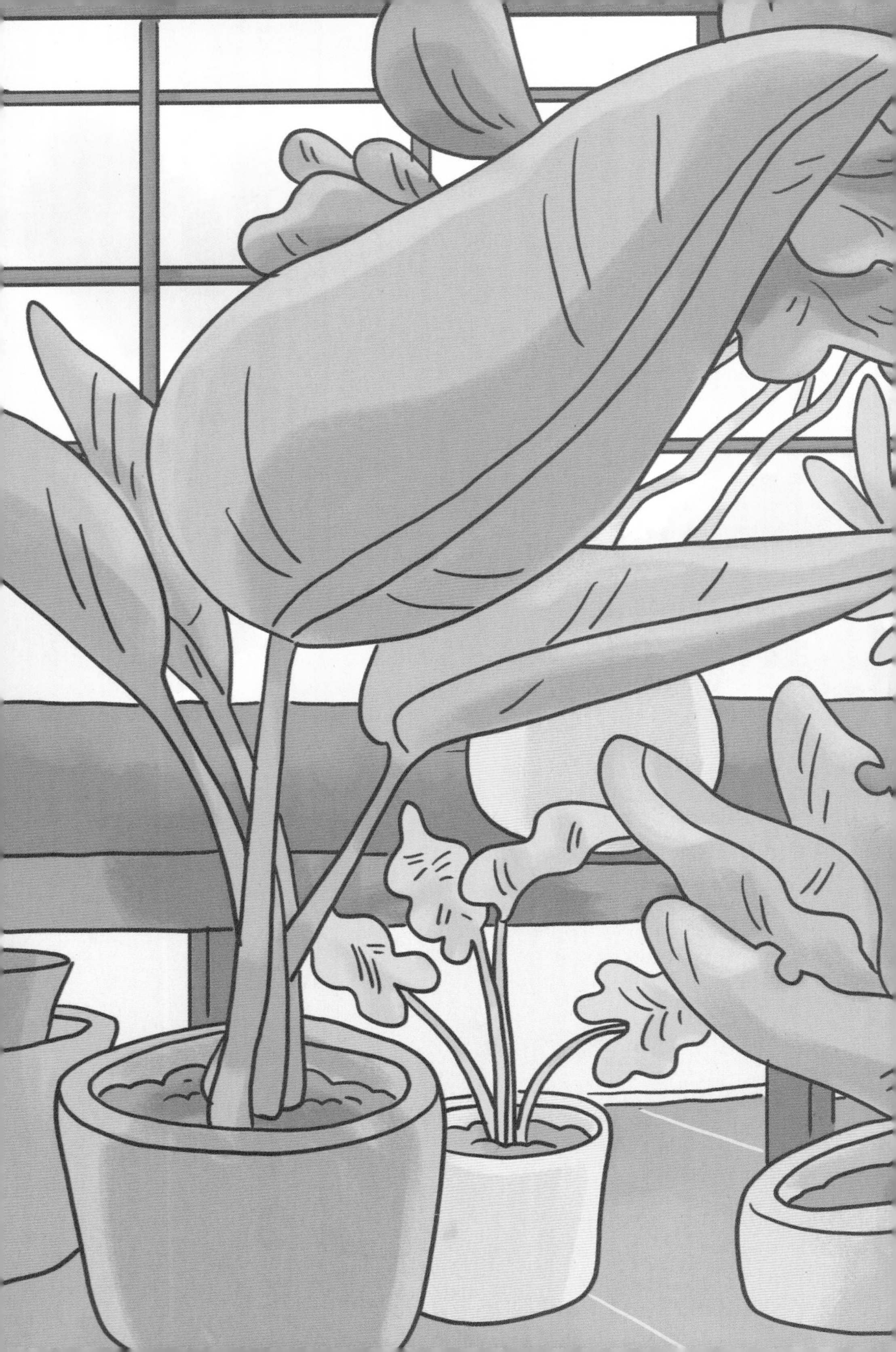

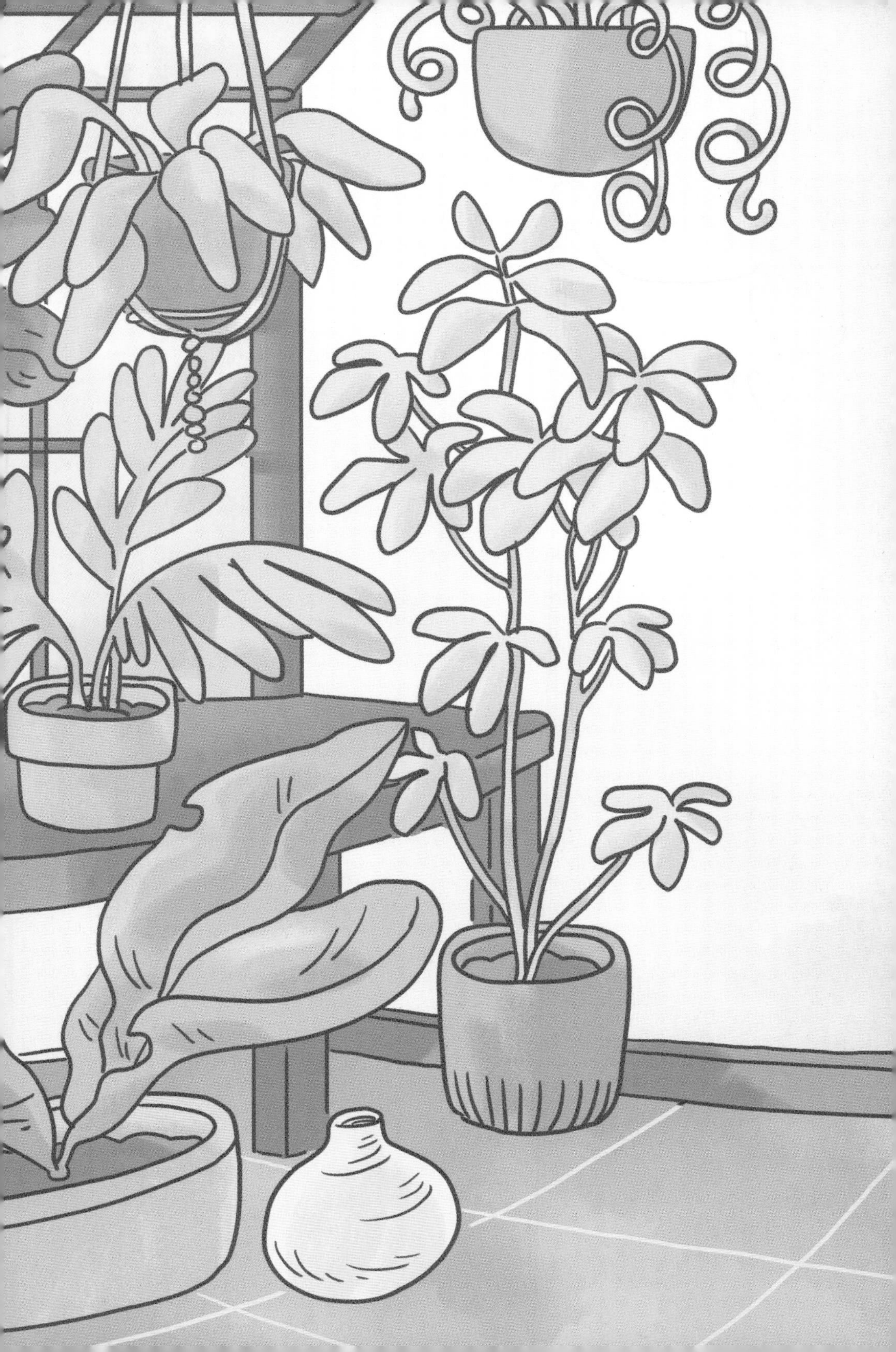

To Emi!

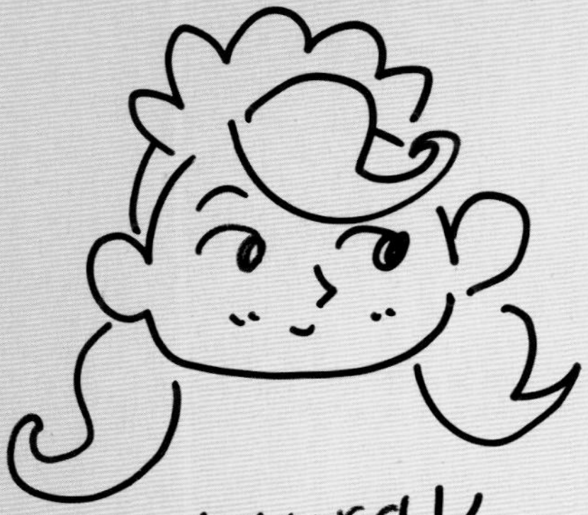

♡laurak

I LIKE TO READ is a registered trademark of Holiday House Publishing, Inc.

HOLIDAY HOUSE is registered in the U.S. Patent and Trademark Office.
Printed and bound in April 2021 at Leo Paper, Heshan, China.
The art was created digitally.
www.holidayhouse.com
3 5 7 9 10 8 6 4 2

Library of Congress Cataloging-in-Publication Data

Names: Knetzger, Laura, 1990– author.
Title: Five magic rooms / Laura Knetzger.
Description: New York : Holiday House, [2021] | Series: [I like to read comics] | Audience: Ages 4–8. | Audience: Grades K–1. | Summary: When Mina visits the home of her friend Pie, she is amazed by everything she sees, feels, smells, and tastes, but Pie is sure that her home is just as special.
Identifiers: LCCN 2020052651 | ISBN 9780823444977 (hardcover)
ISBN 9780823450442 (paperback)
Subjects: LCSH: Graphic novels. | CYAC: Graphic novels.
Dwellings—Fiction. | Friendship—Fiction.
Classification: LCC PZ7.7.K655 Fiv 2021 | DDC 741.5/973—dc23
LC record available at https://lccn.loc.gov/2020052651

ISBN: 978-0-8234-4497-7 (hardcover)
ISBN: 978-0-8234-5044-2 (paperback)

FiVe MAGIC ROOMS

LAURA KNETZGER

HOLIDAY HOUSE · NEW YORK

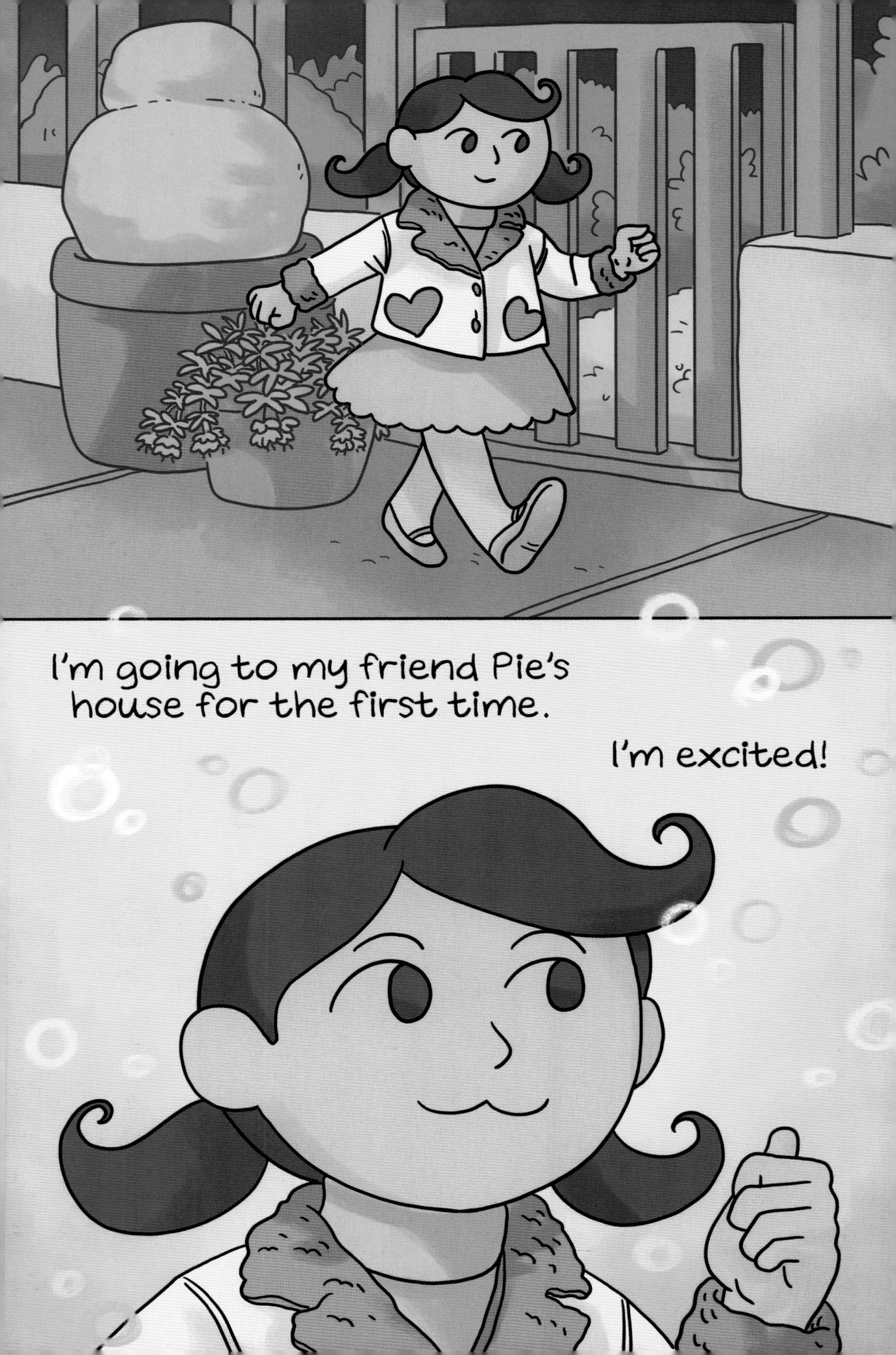
I'm going to my friend Pie's house for the first time.
I'm excited!

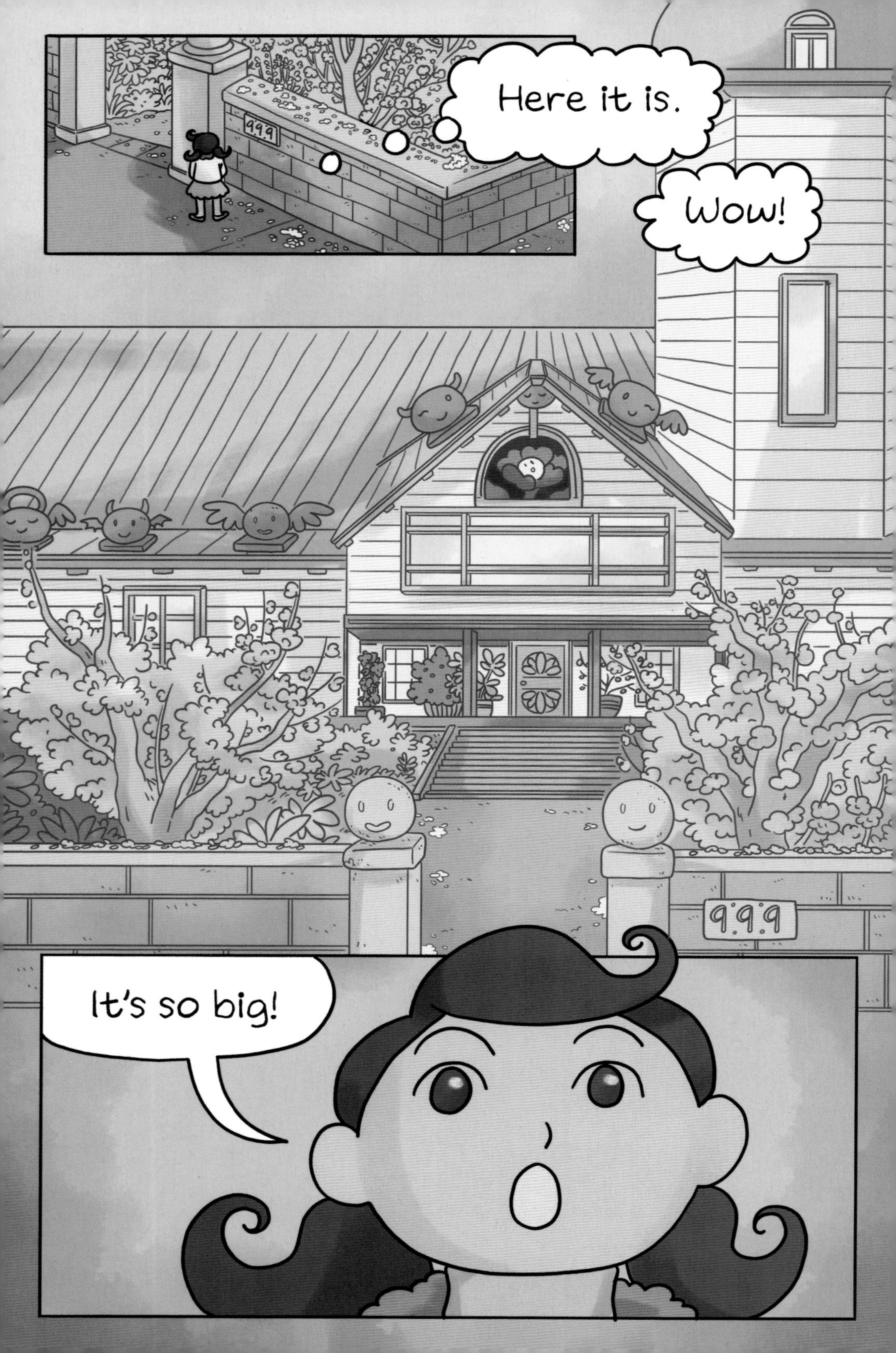
Here it is.
999
Wow!
999
It's so big!

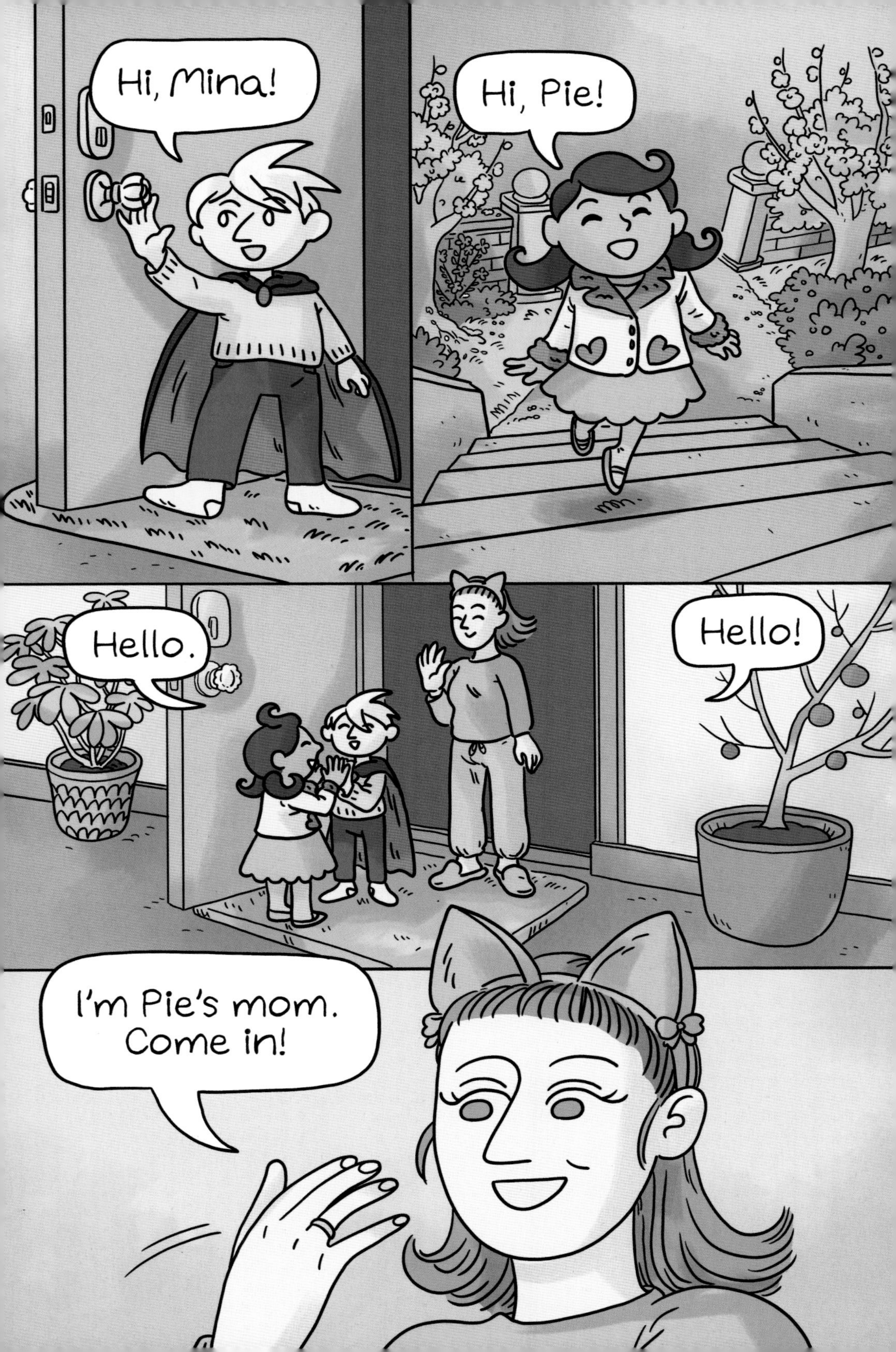
Hi, Mina!
Hi, Pie!
Hello.
Hello!
I'm Pie's mom.
Come in!

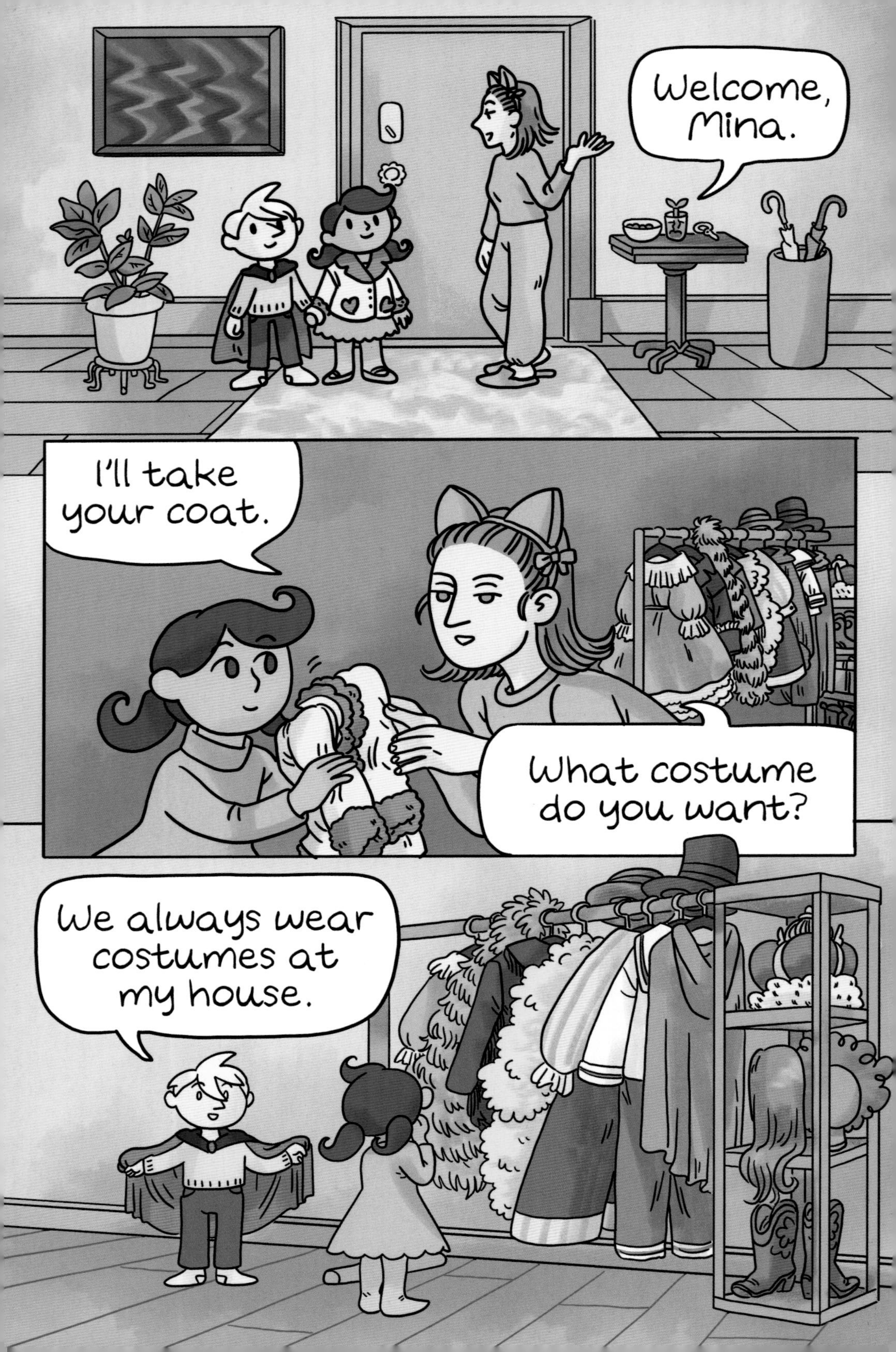
Welcome, Mina.
I'll take your coat.
What costume do you want?
We always wear costumes at my house.

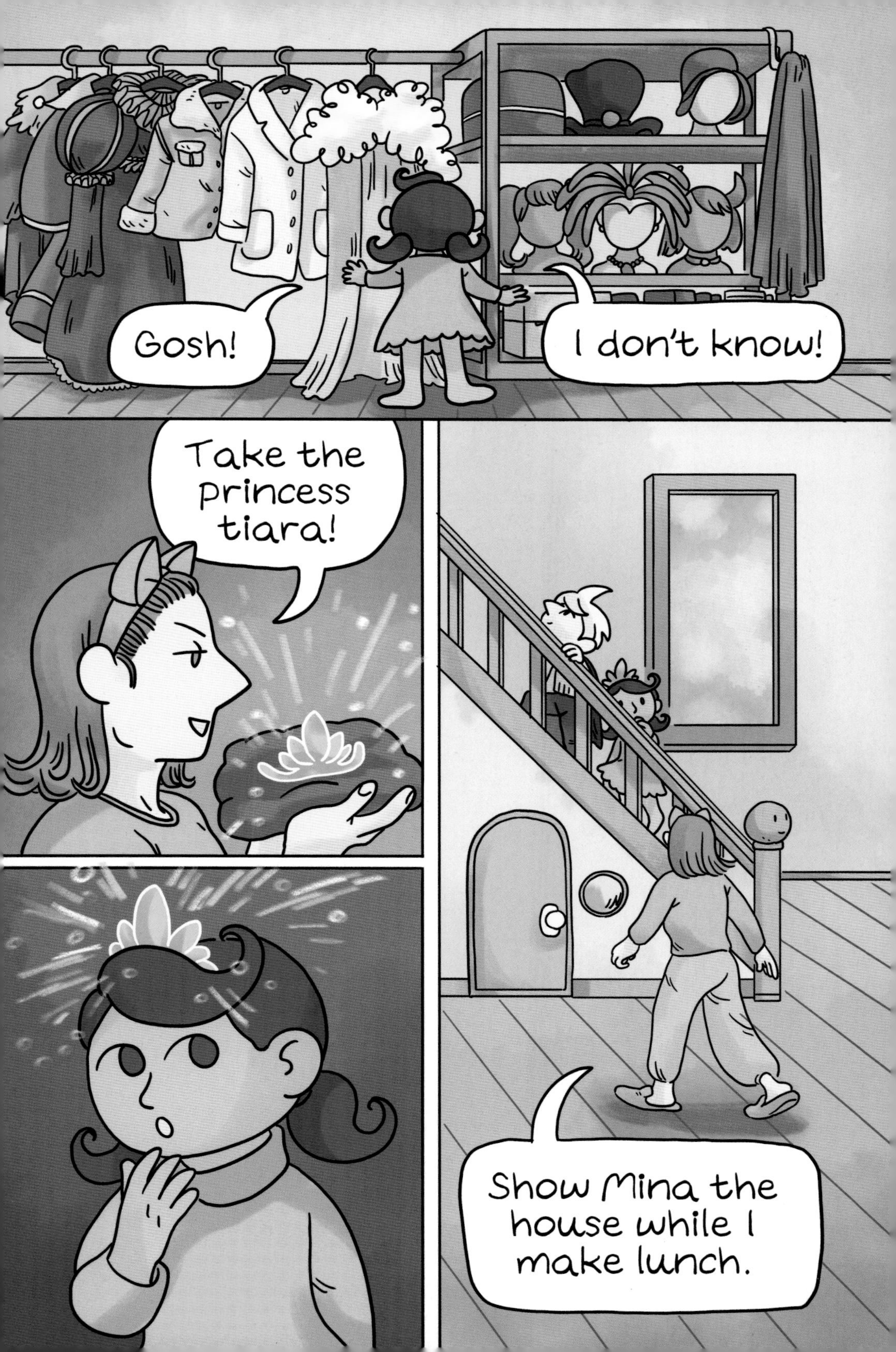
Gosh!
I don't know!
Take the princess tiara!
Show Mina the house while I make lunch.

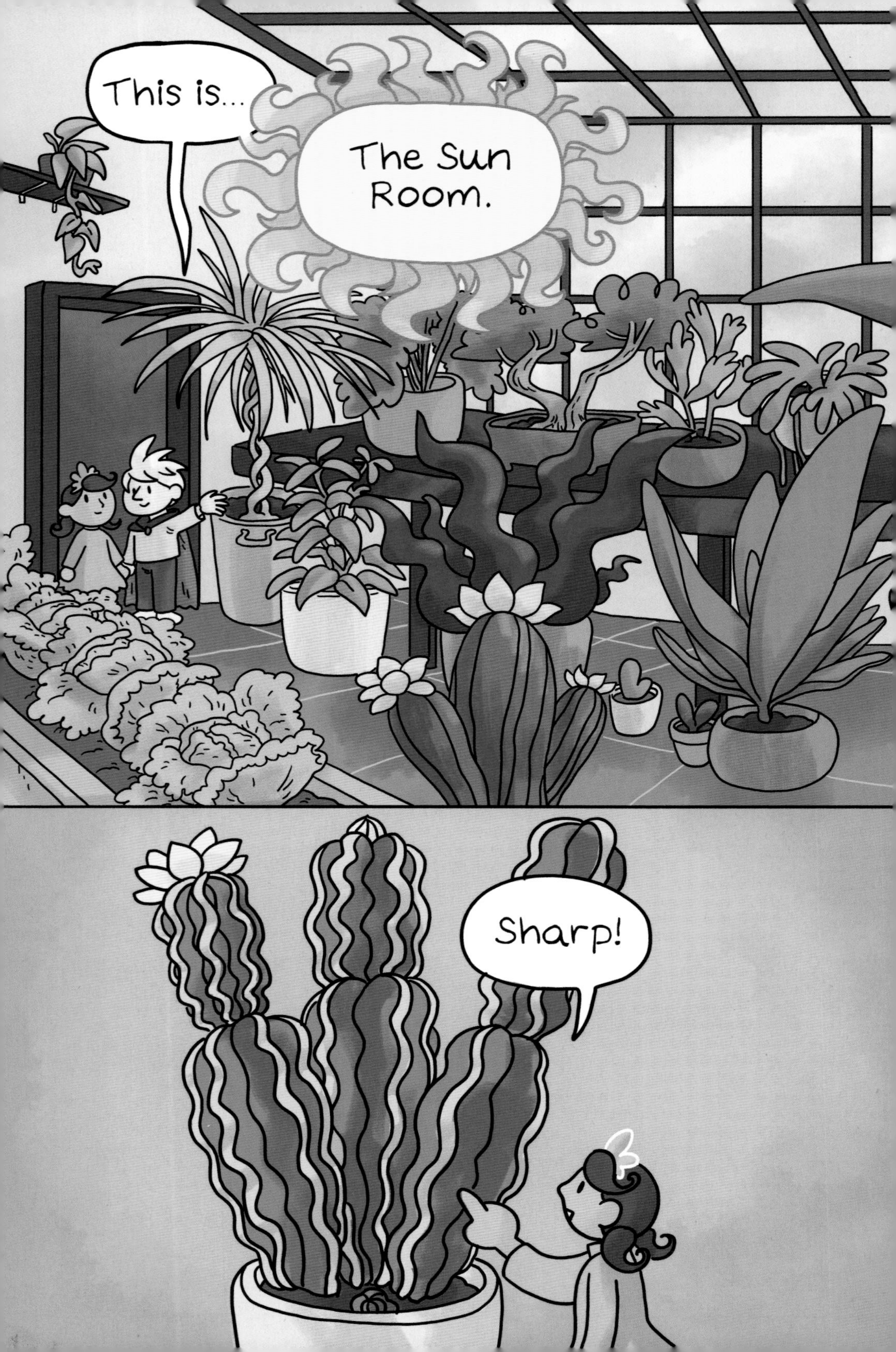
This is...
The Sun Room.
Sharp!

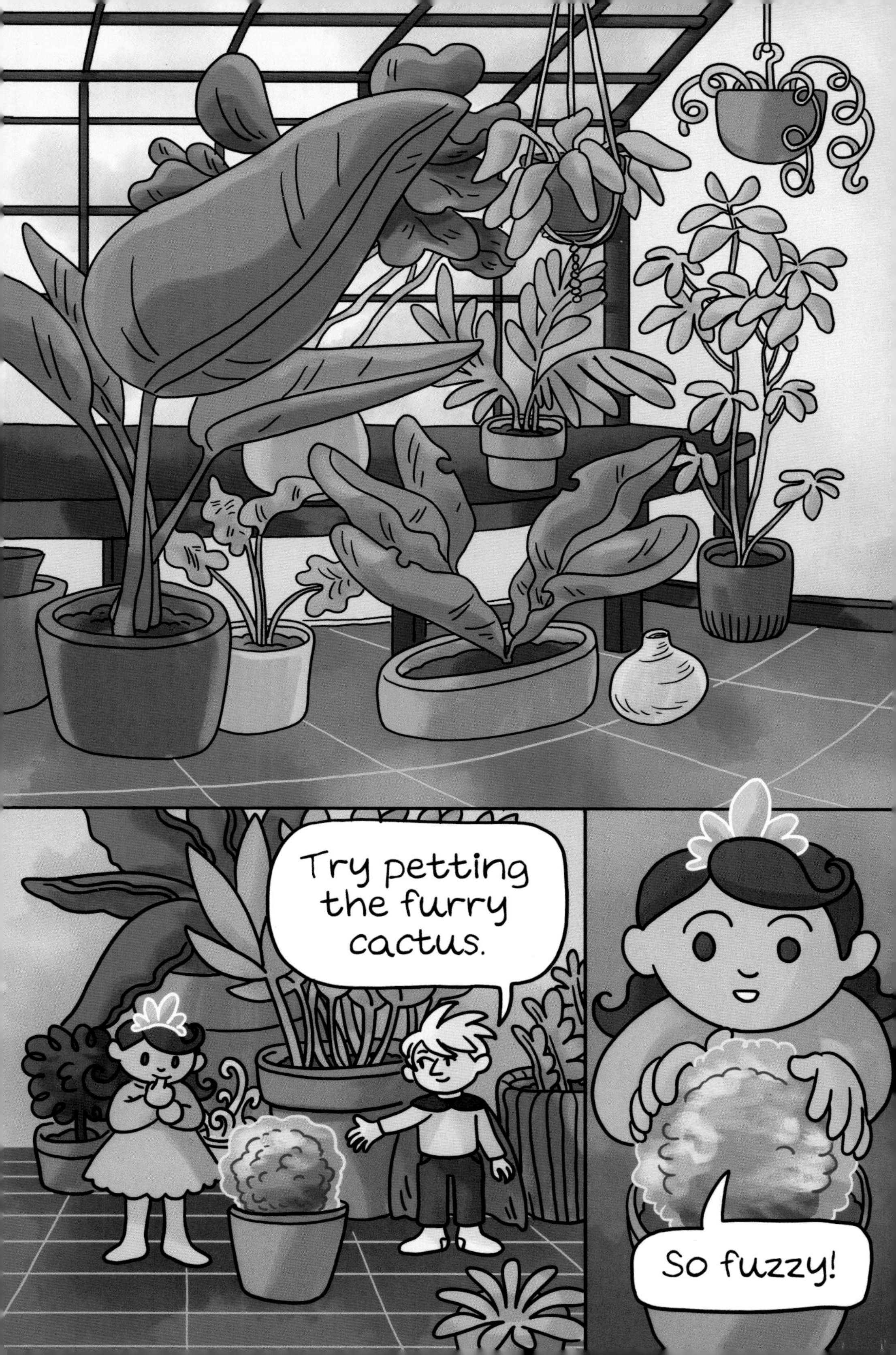
Try petting the furry cactus.
So fuzzy!

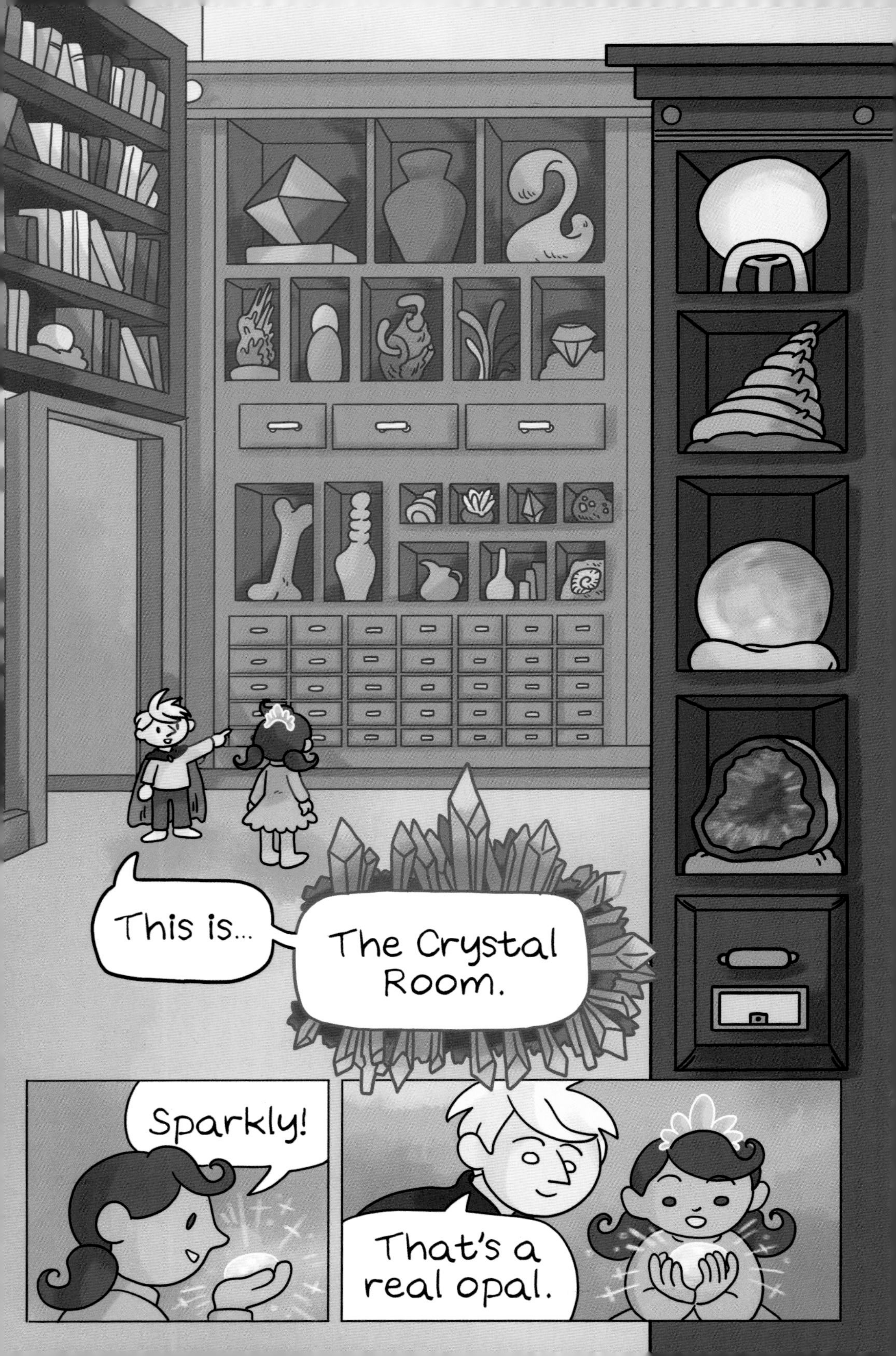
This is...
The Crystal Room.
Sparkly!
That's a real opal.

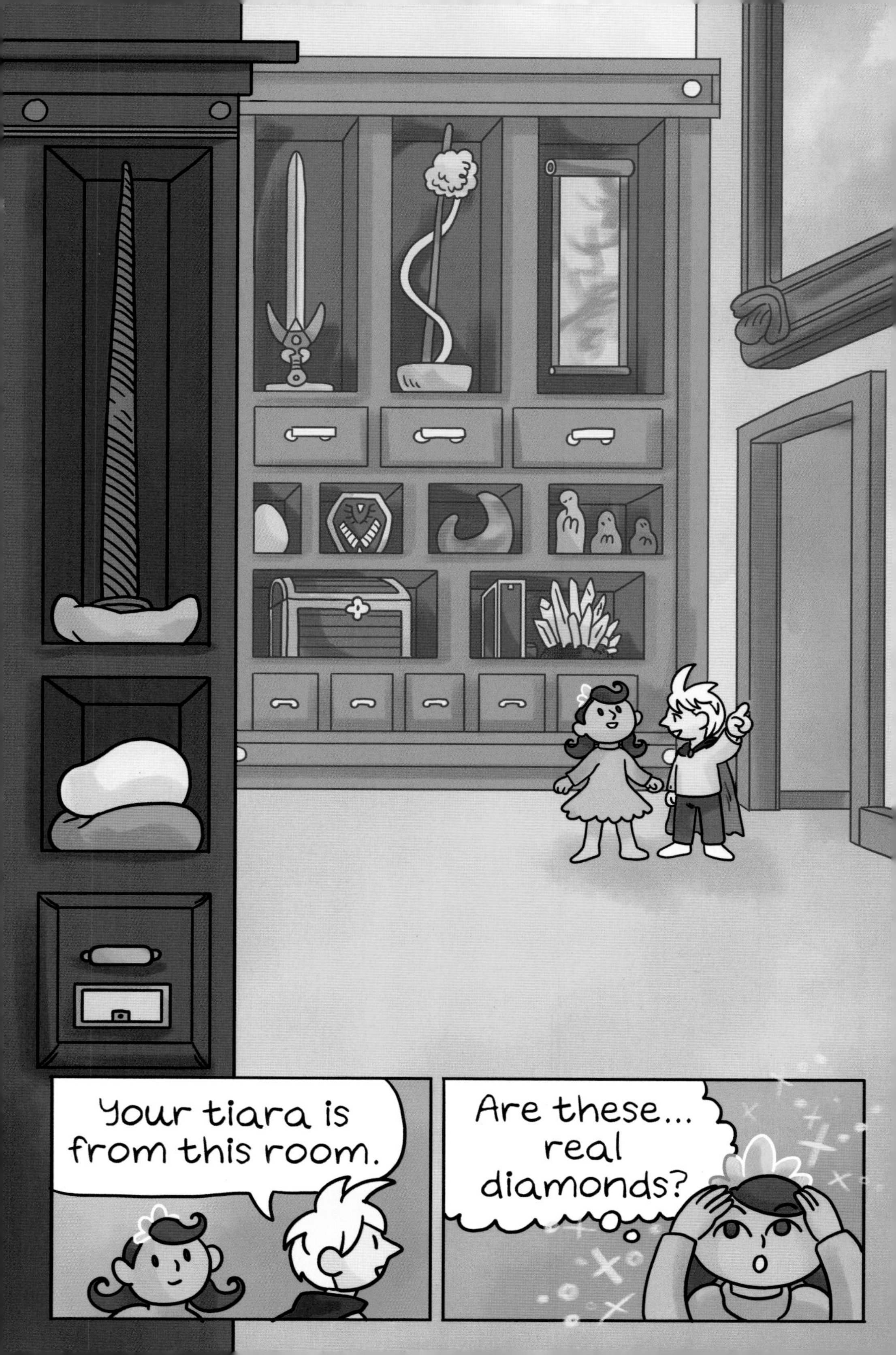
Your tiara is from this room.
Are these... real diamonds?

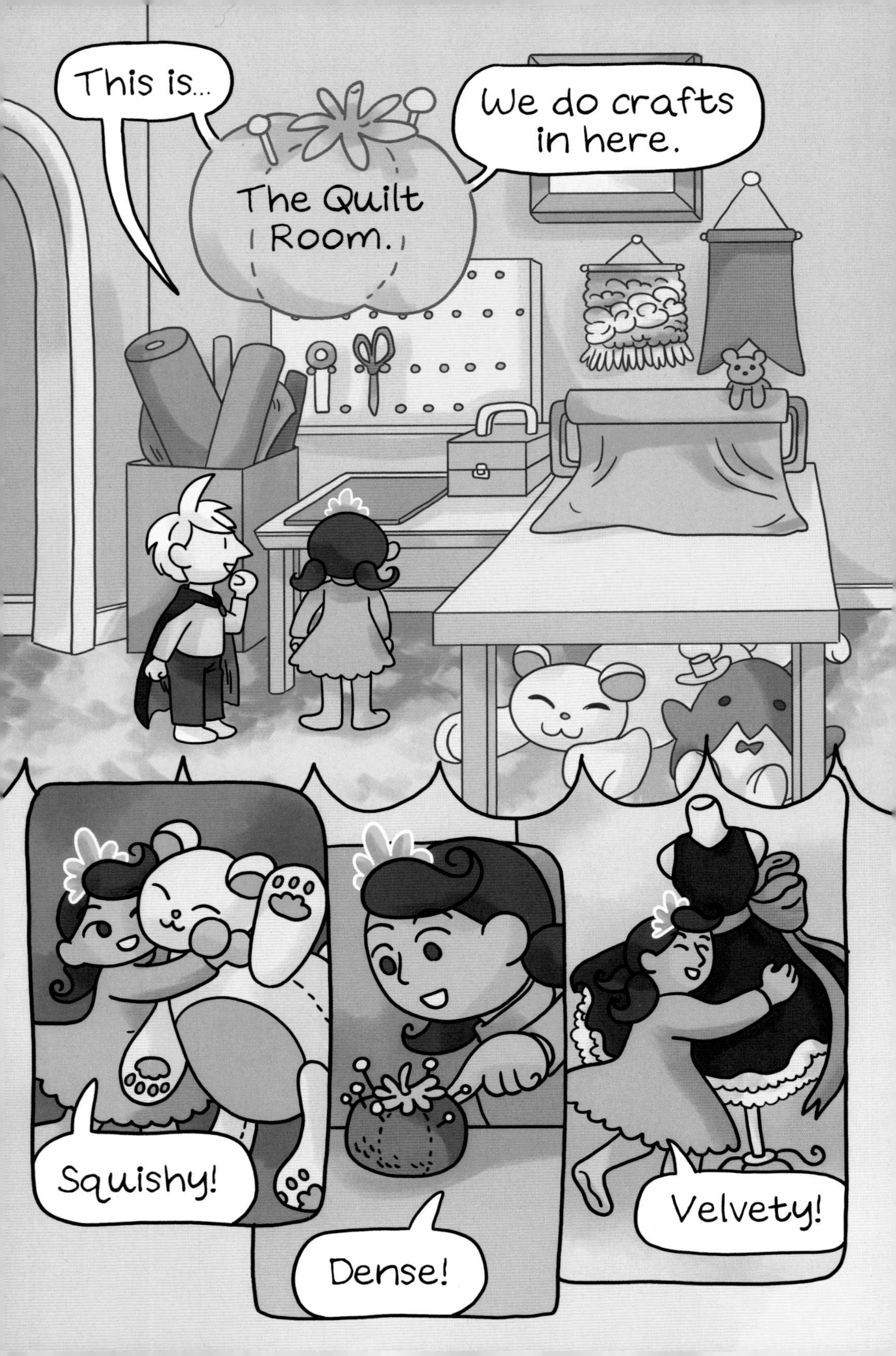
This is...
The Quilt Room.
We do crafts in here.
Squishy!
Dense!
Velvety!

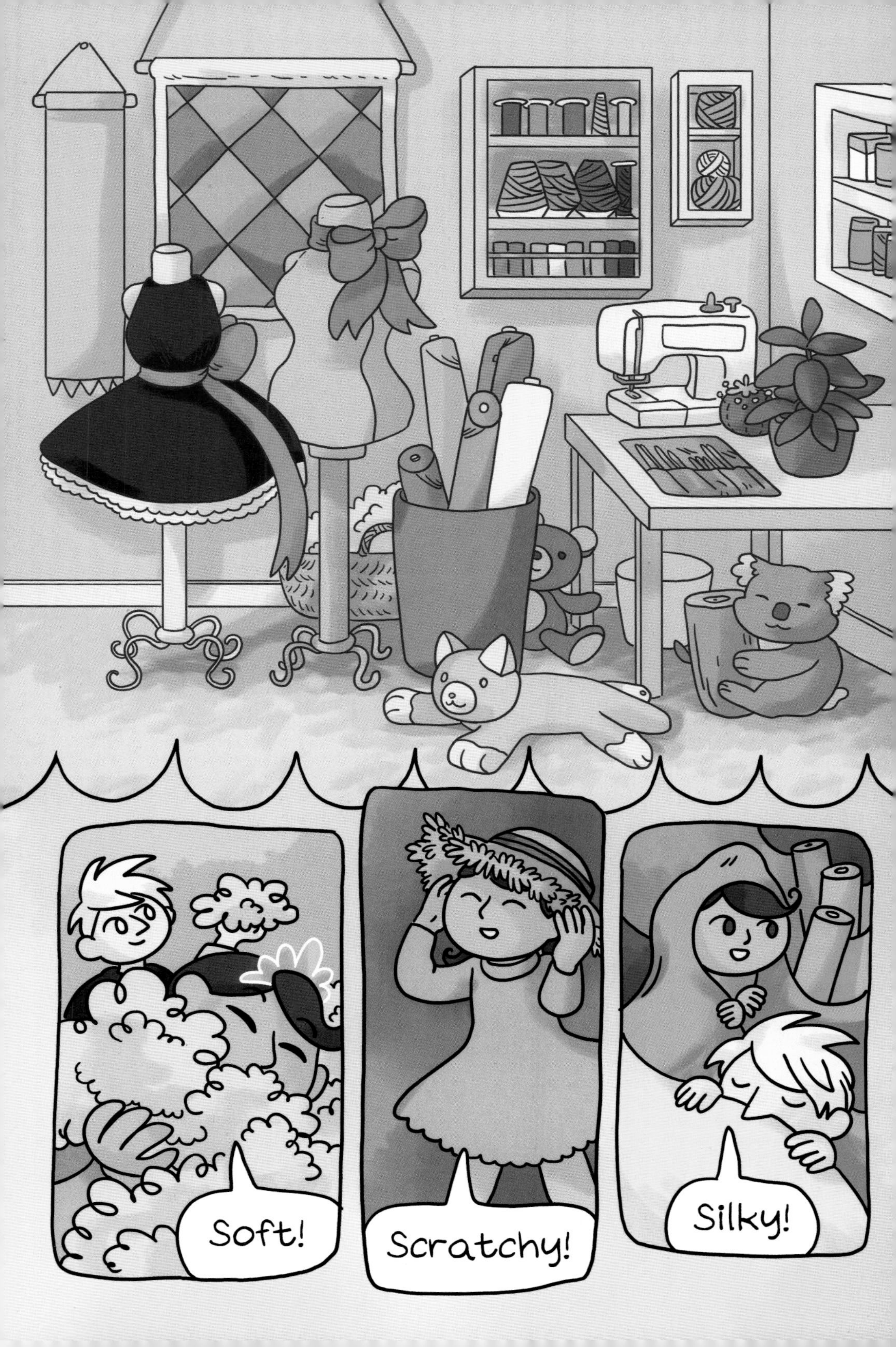
Soft!
Scratchy!
Silky!

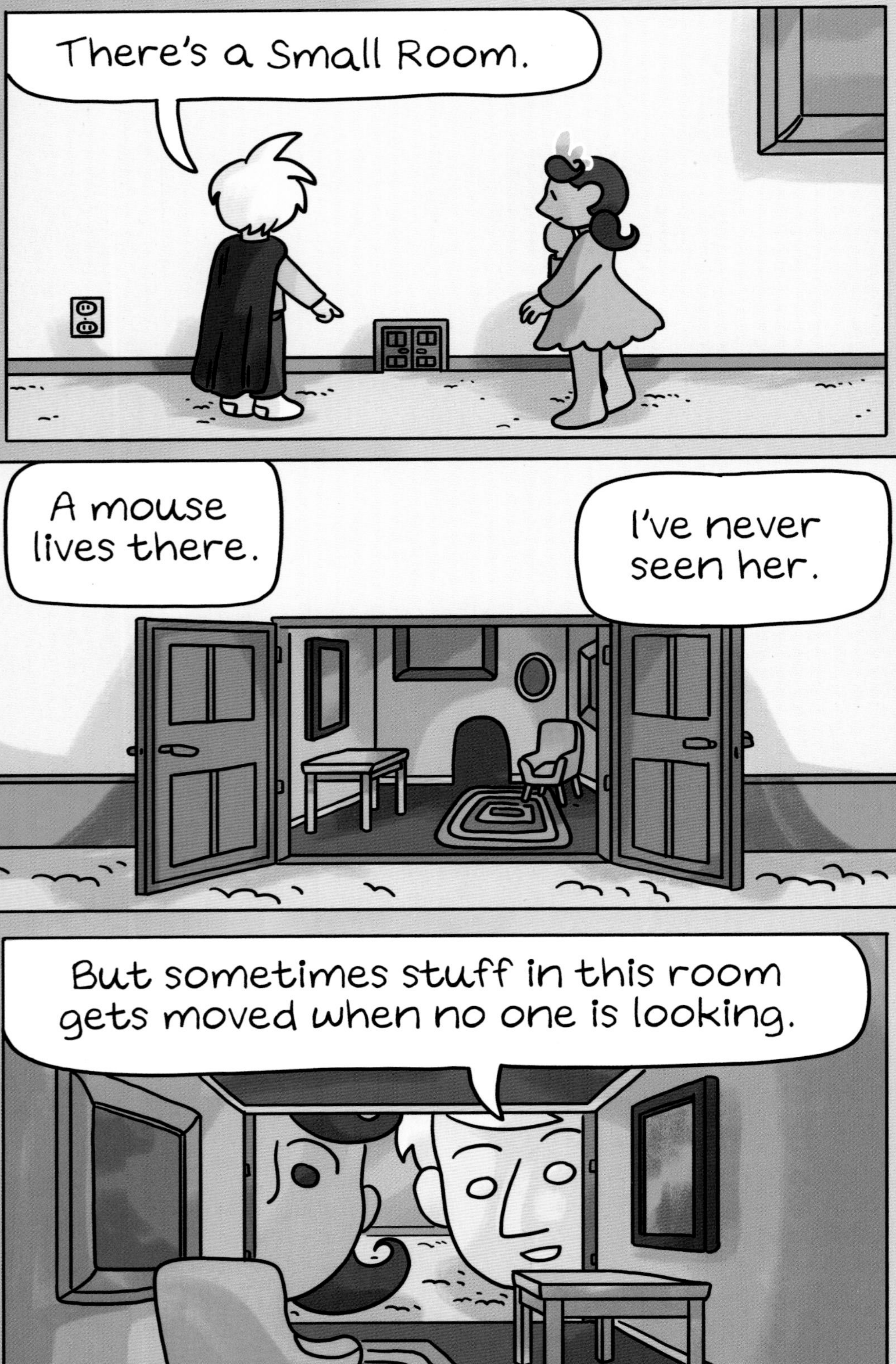
There's a Small Room.
A mouse lives there.
I've never seen her.
But sometimes stuff in this room gets moved when no one is looking.

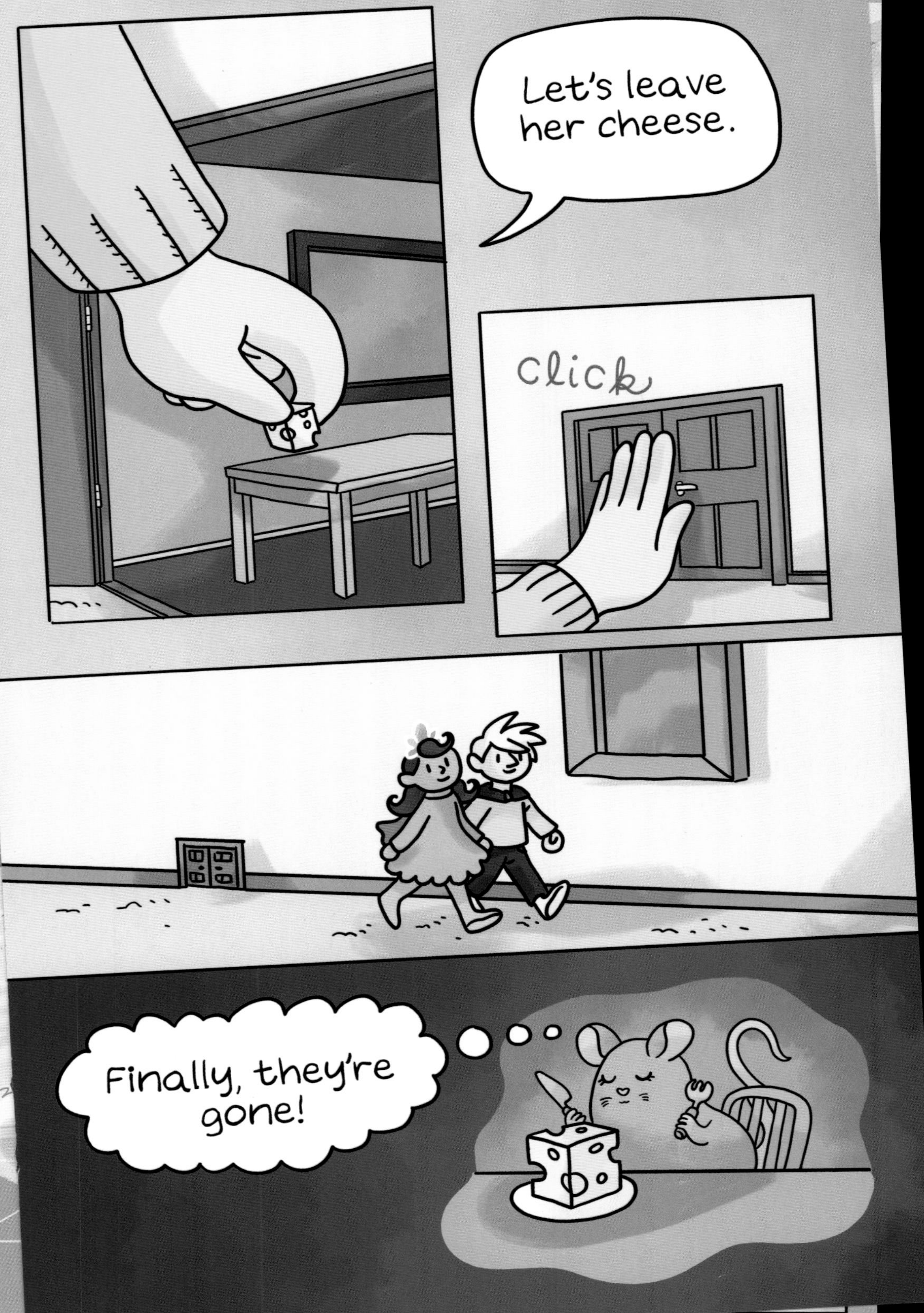
Let's leave her cheese.
Click
Finally, they're gone!

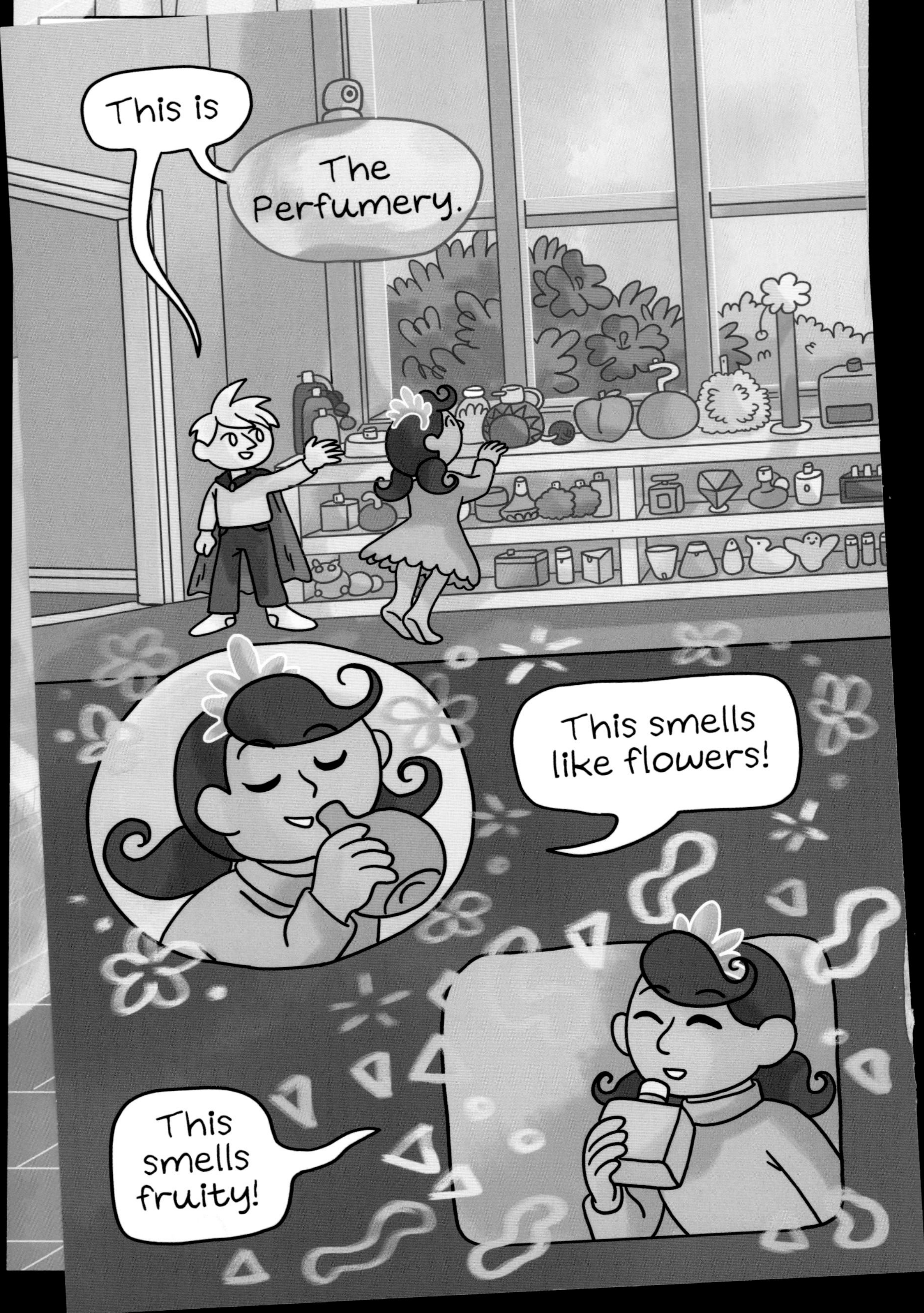
This is
The Perfumery.
This smells like flowers!
This smells fruity!

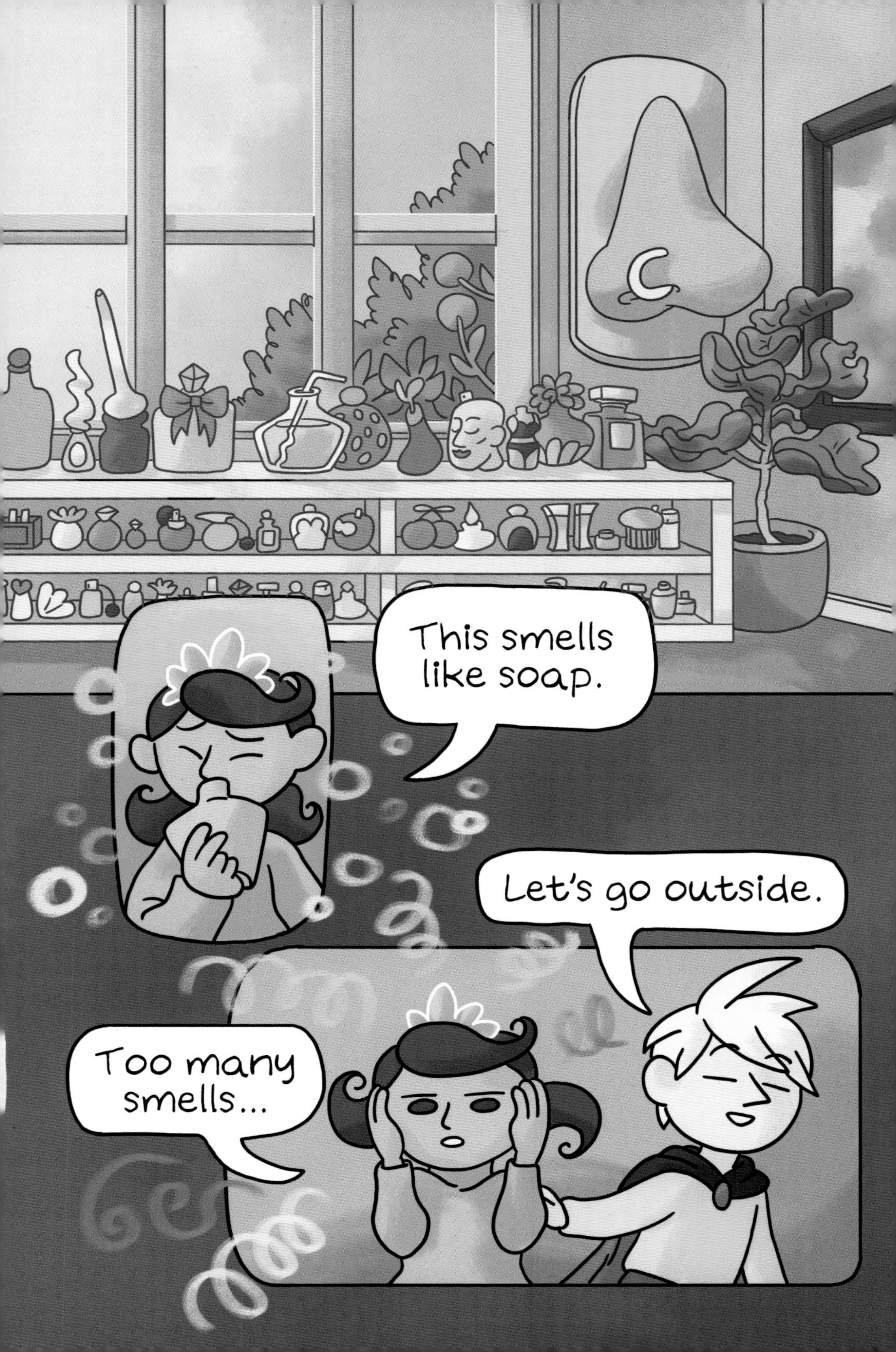
This smells like soap.
Let's go outside.
Too many smells...

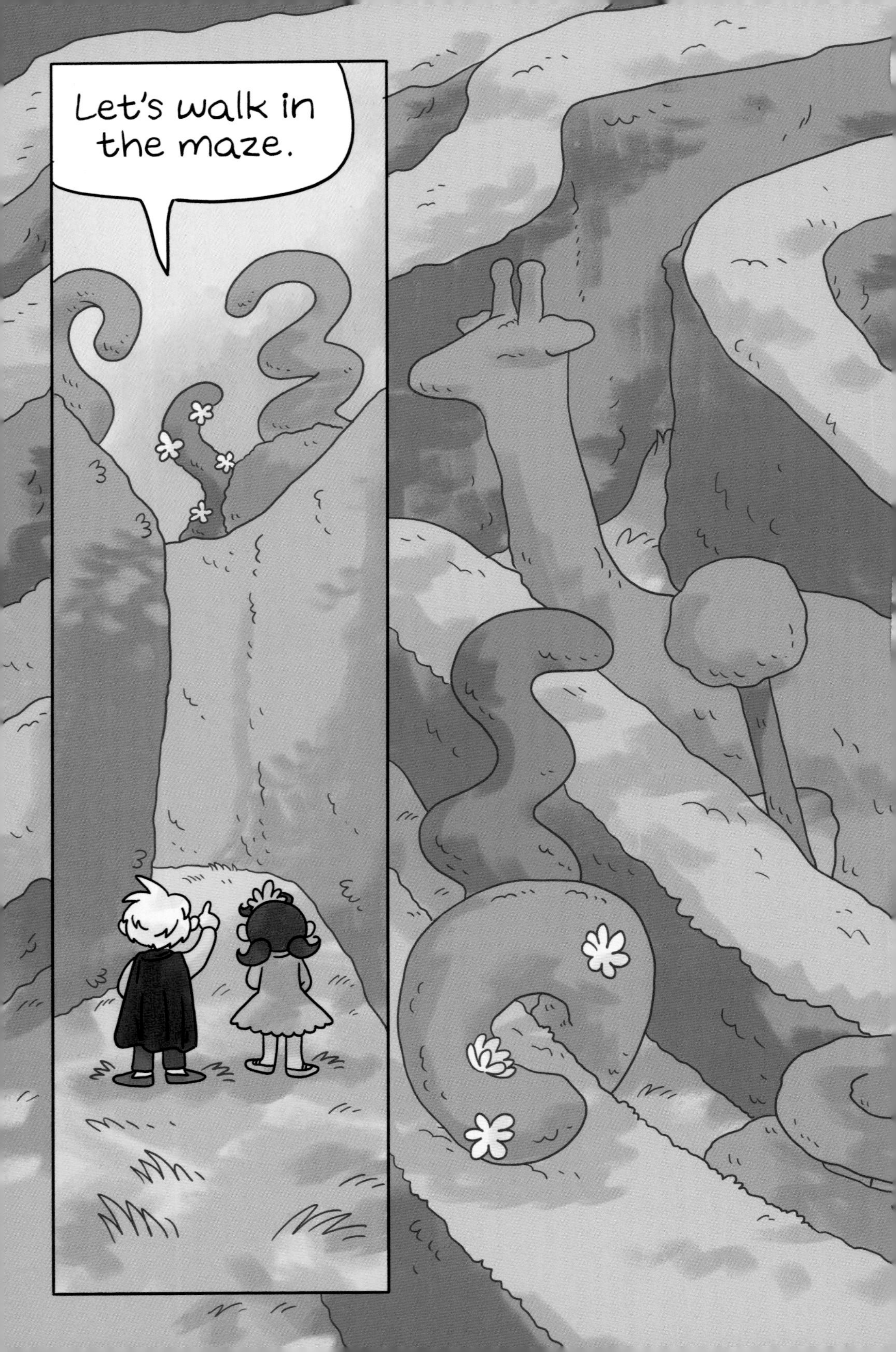
Let's walk in the maze.

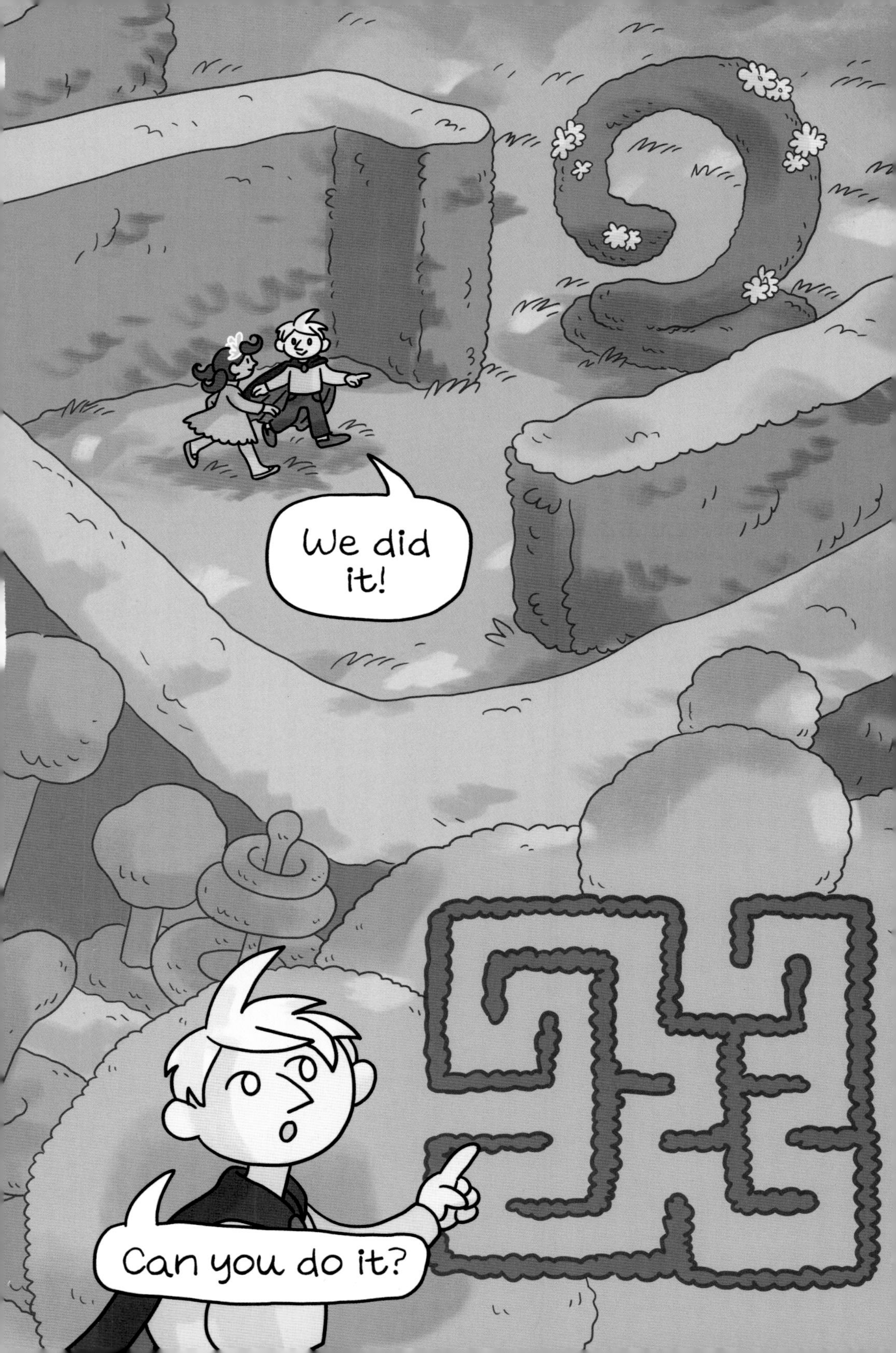
We did it!
Can you do it?

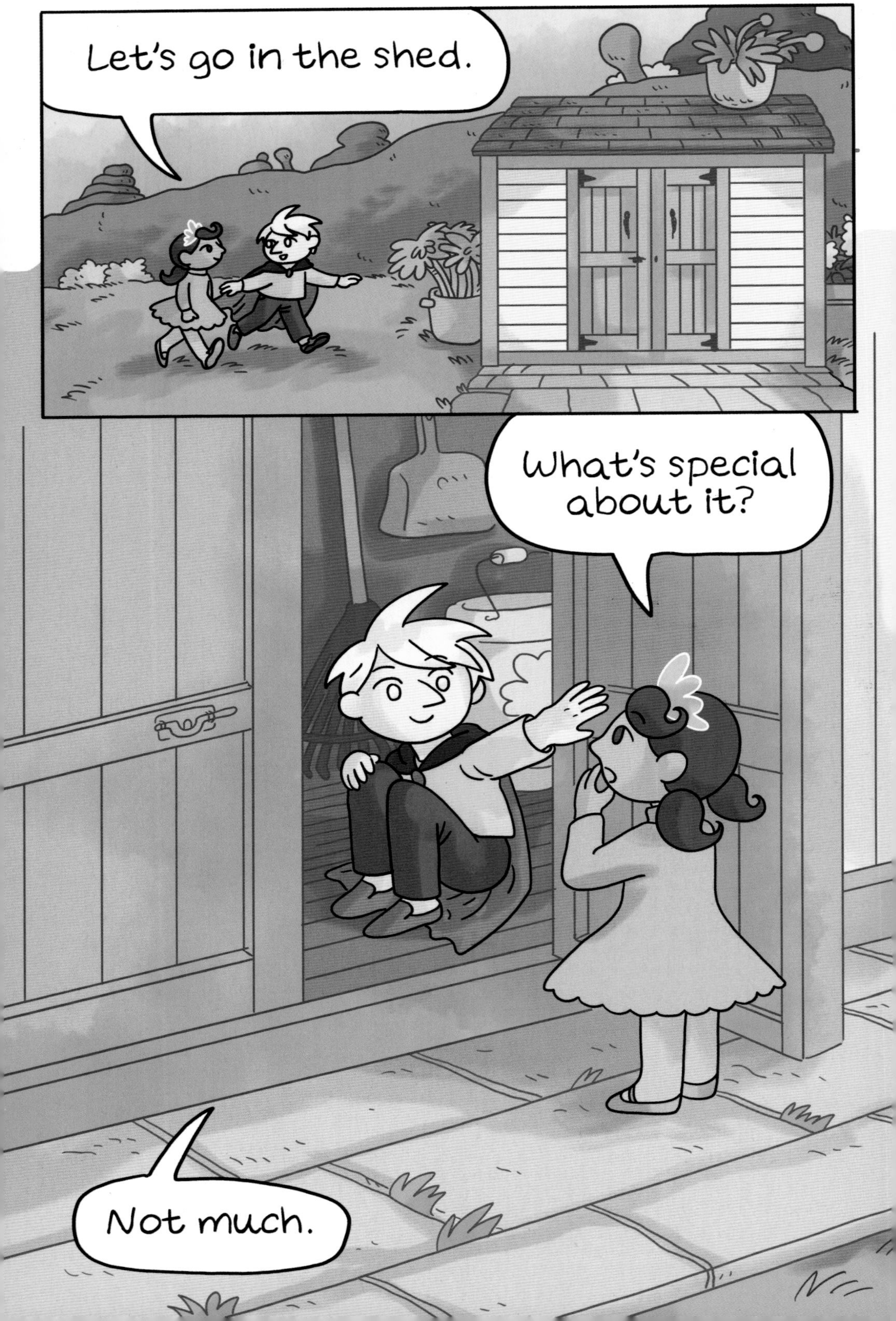
Let's go in the shed.
What's special about it?
Not much.

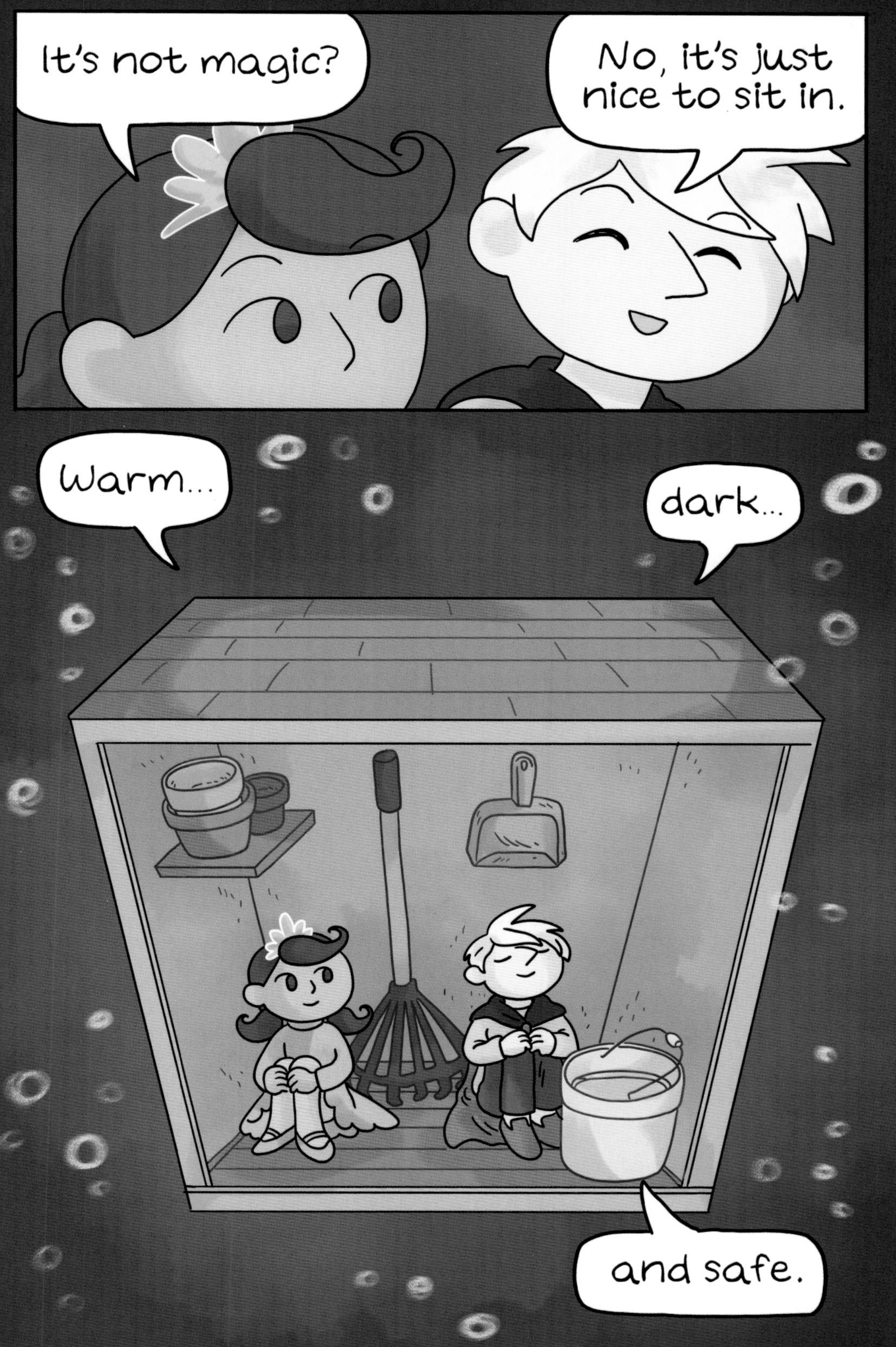
It's not magic?
No, it's just nice to sit in.
Warm...
dark...
and safe.

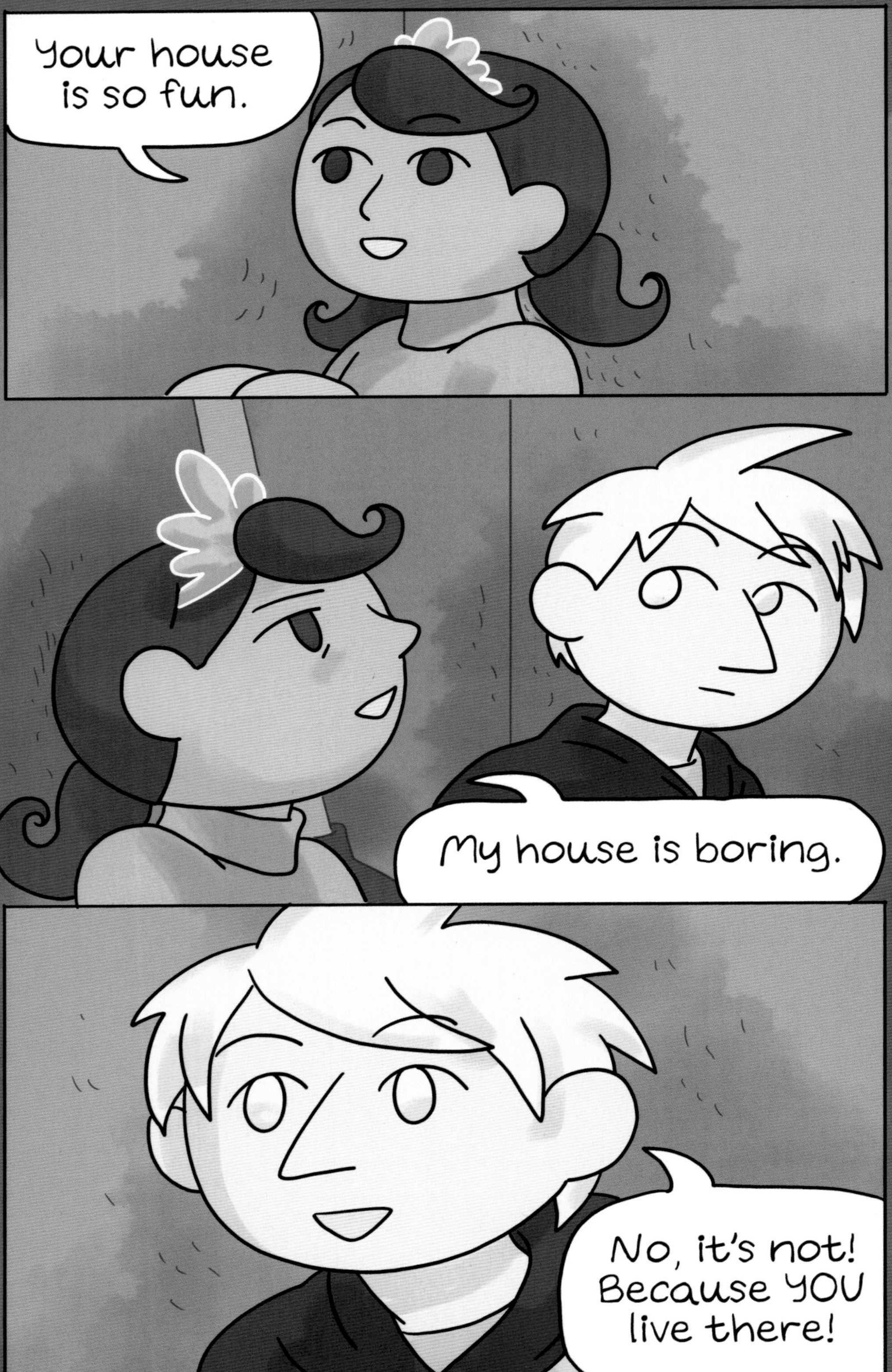
Your house is so fun.
My house is boring.
No, it's not! Because YOU live there!

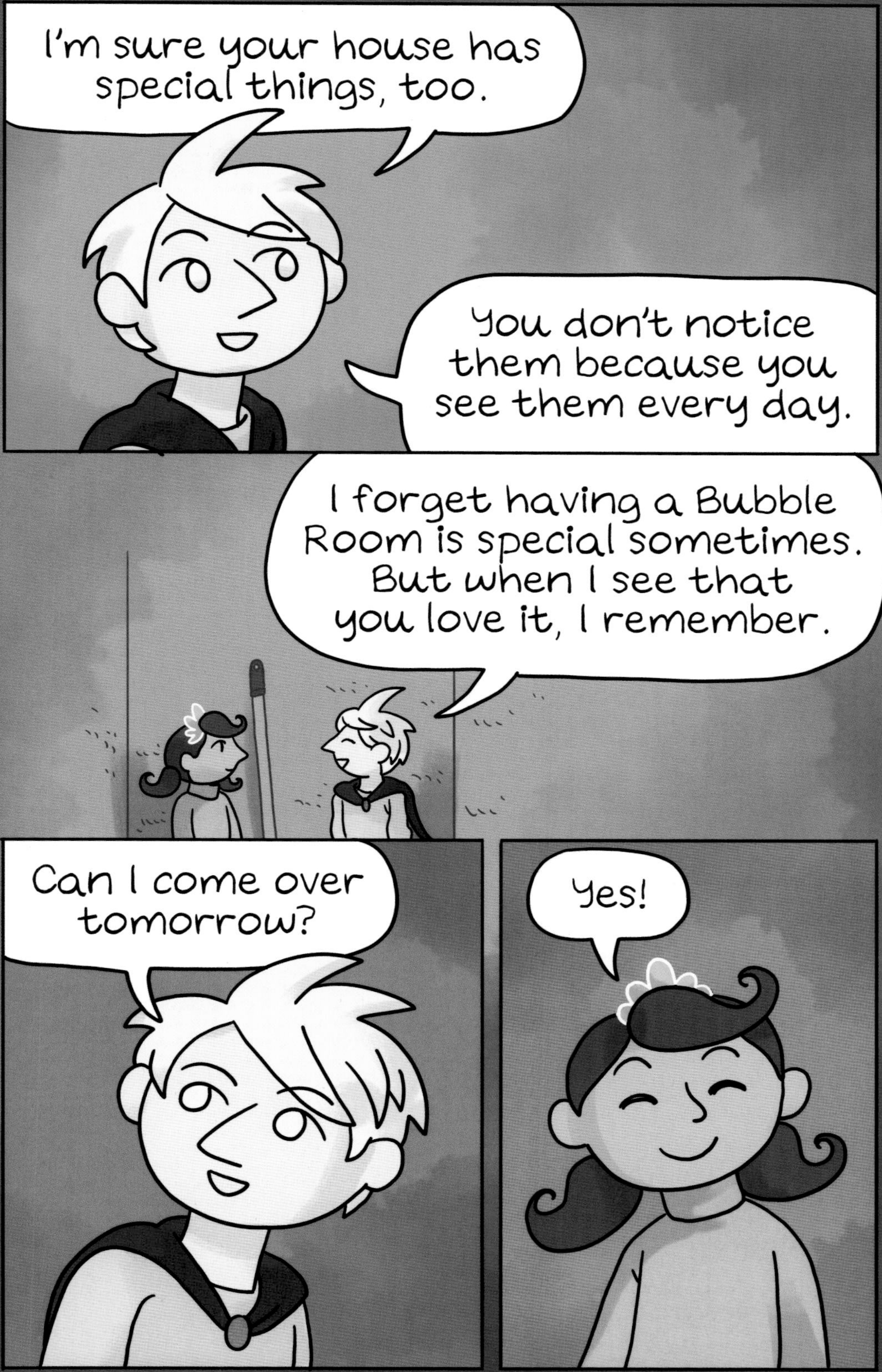
I'm sure your house has special things, too.
You don't notice them because you see them every day.
I forget having a Bubble Room is special sometimes. But when I see that you love it, I remember.
Can I come over tomorrow?
Yes!

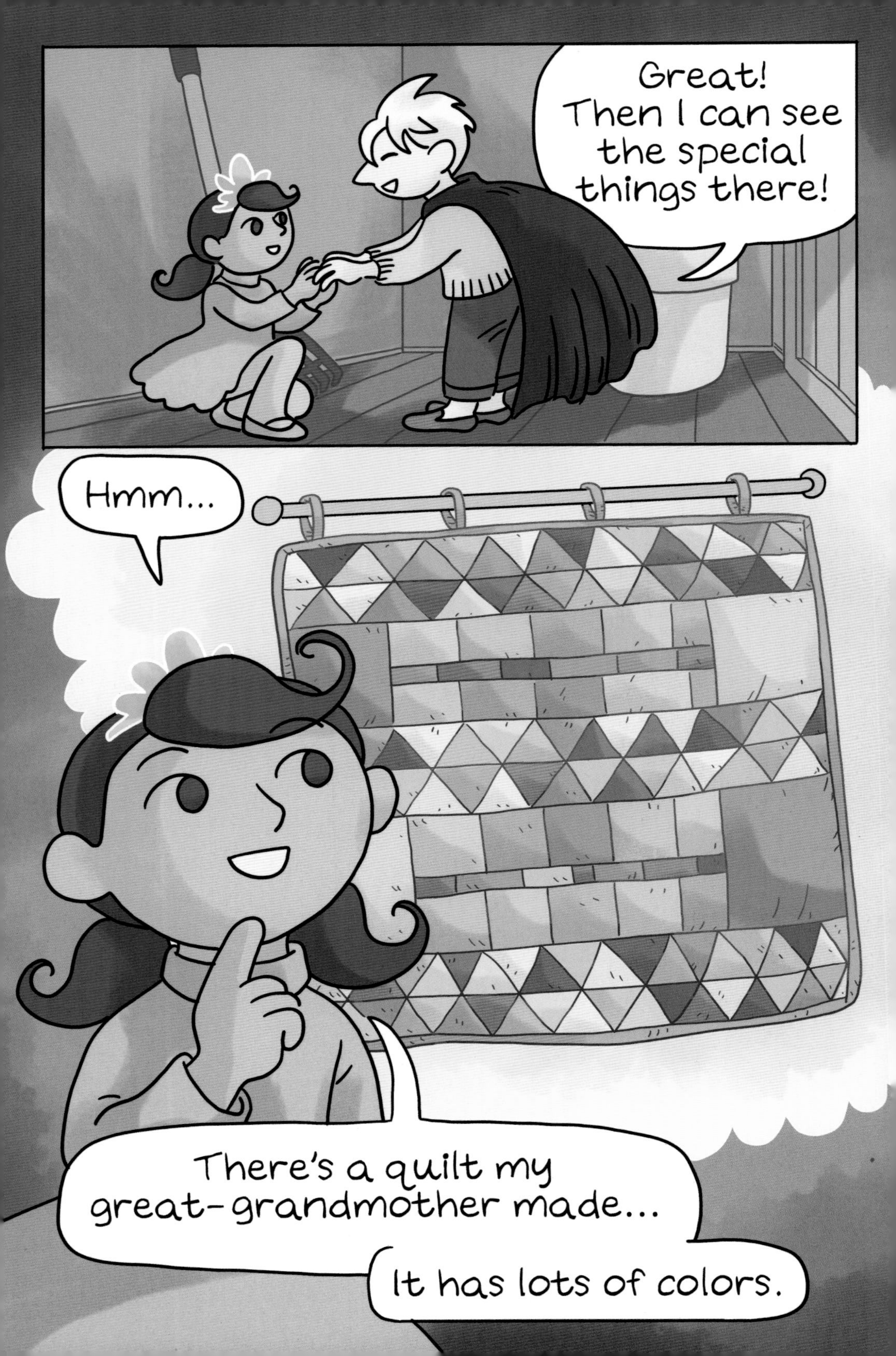
Great! Then I can see the special things there!
Hmm...
There's a quilt my great-grandmother made...
It has lots of colors.

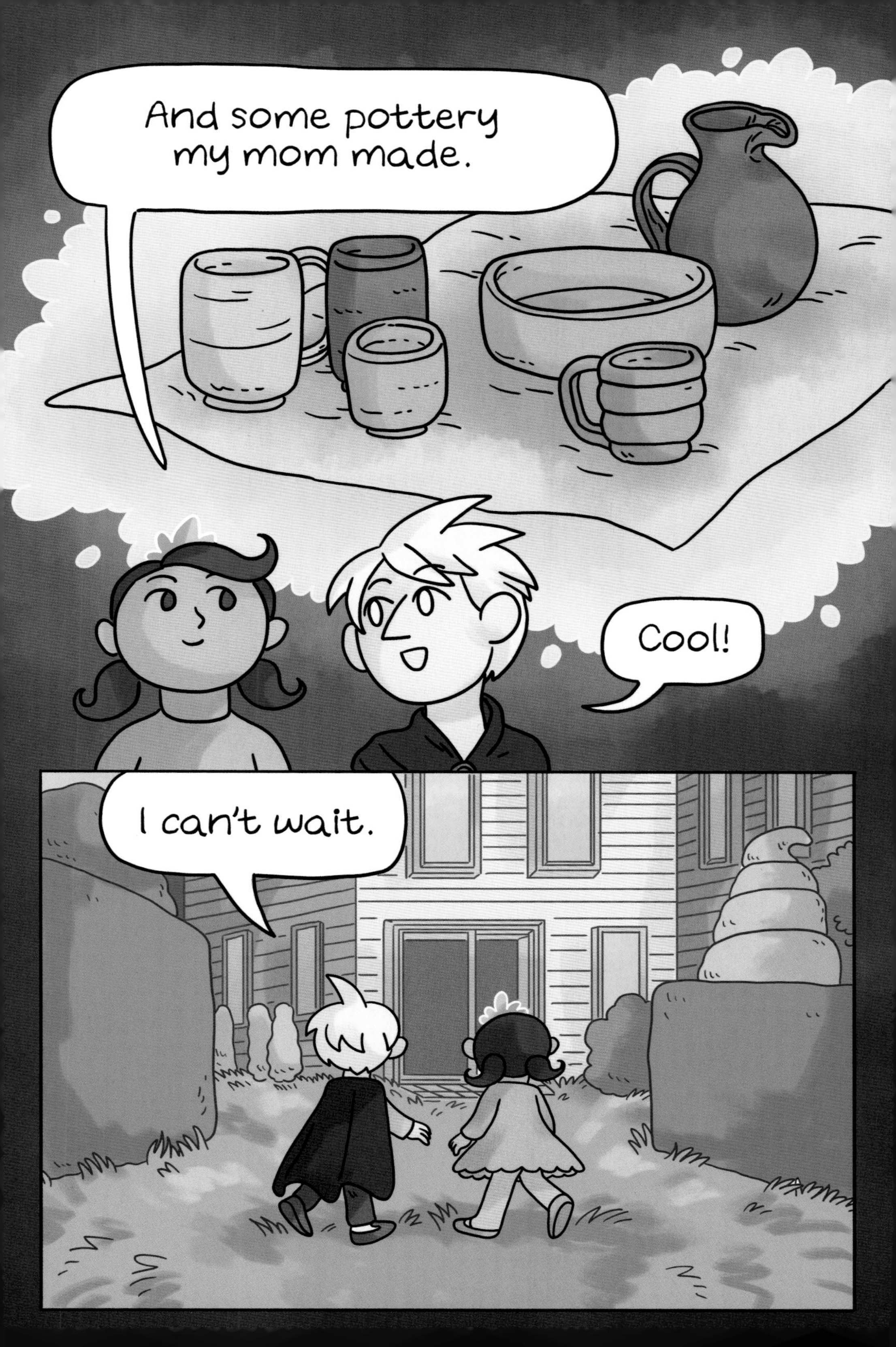
And some pottery
my mom made.
Cool!
I can't wait.

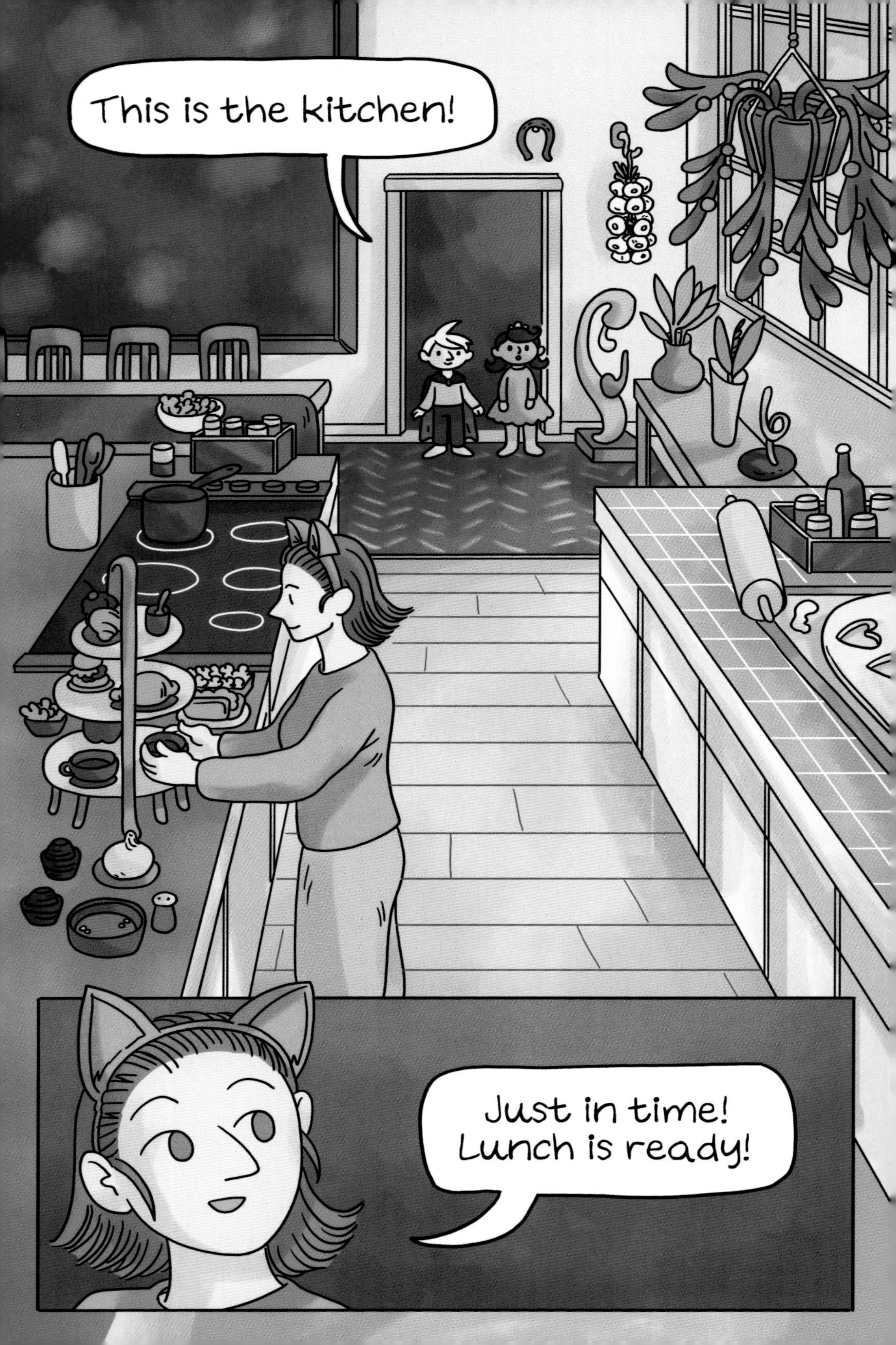
This is the kitchen!
Just in time! Lunch is ready!

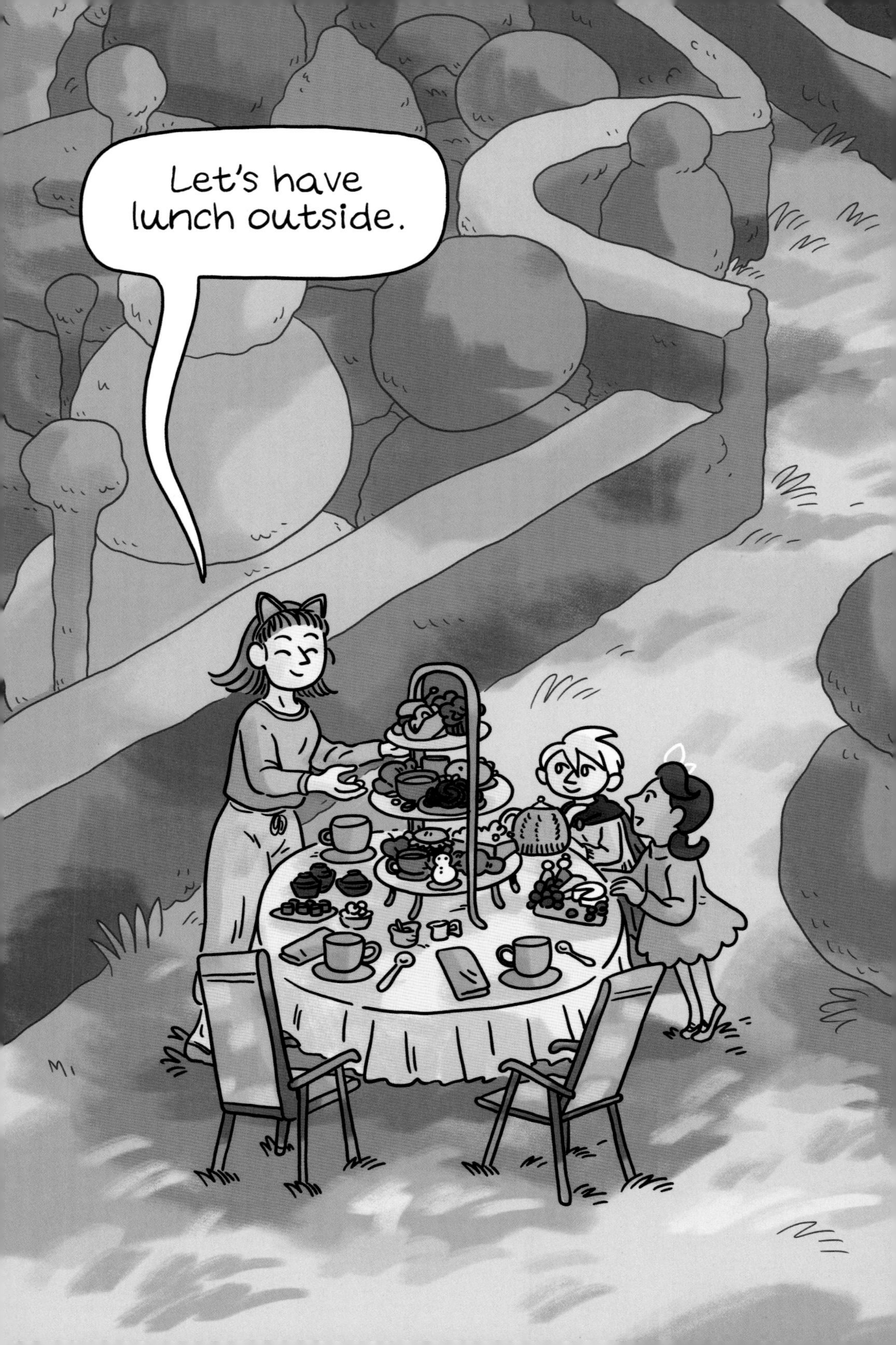
Let's have lunch outside.

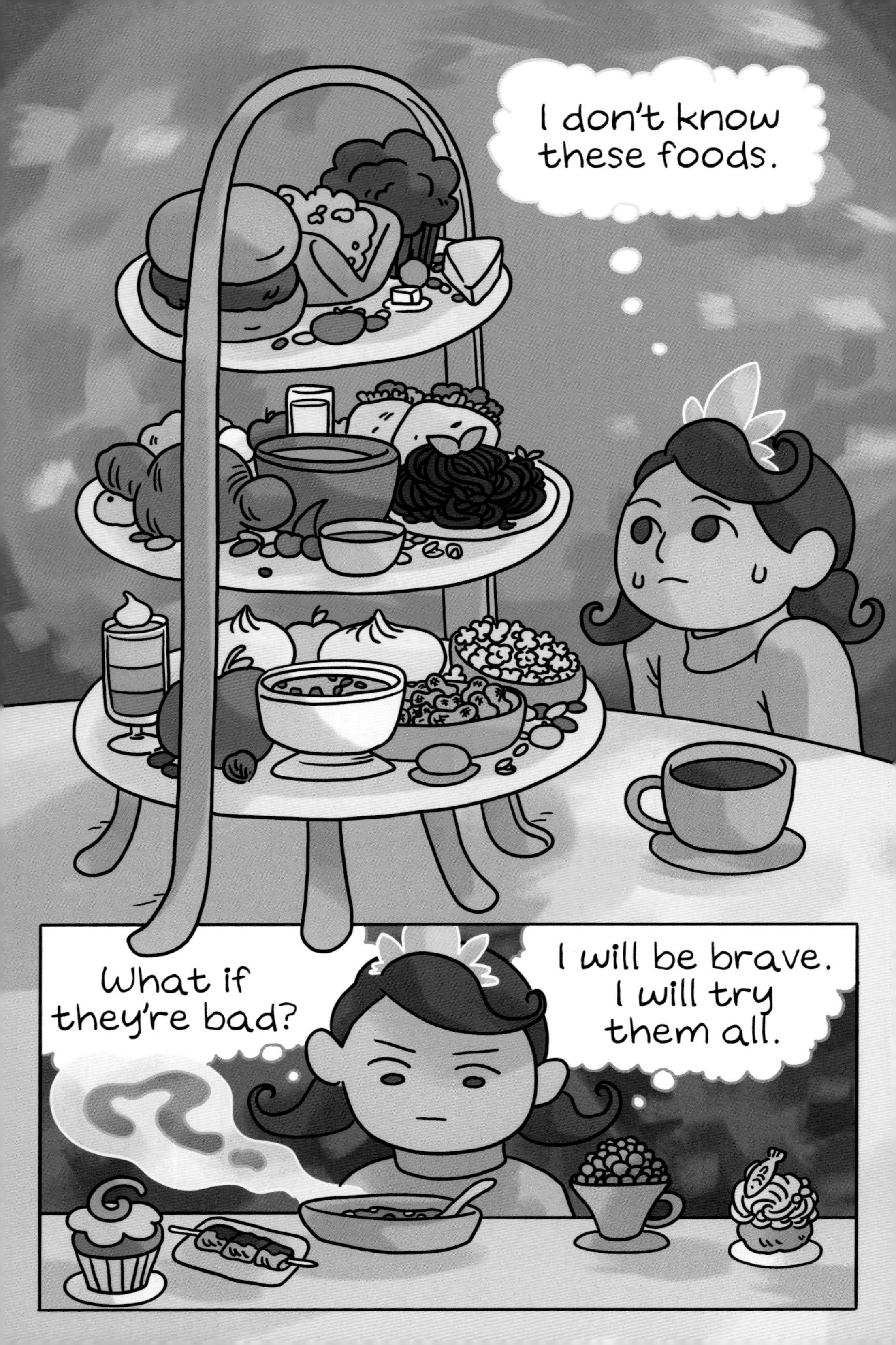
I don't know these foods.
What if they're bad?
I will be brave. I will try them all.

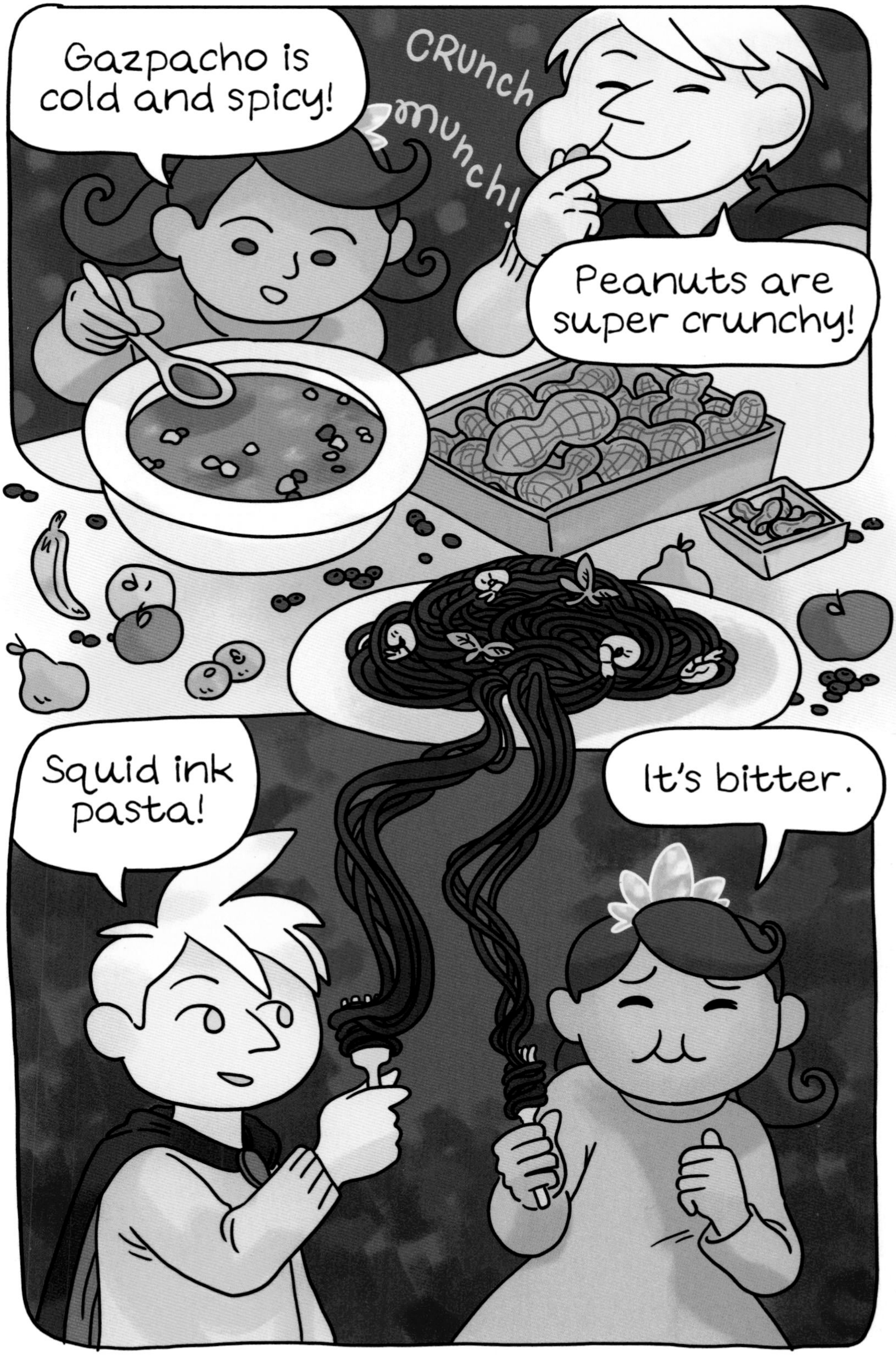
Gazpacho is cold and spicy!
CRUNCH
MUNCH!
Peanuts are super crunchy!
Squid ink pasta!
It's bitter.

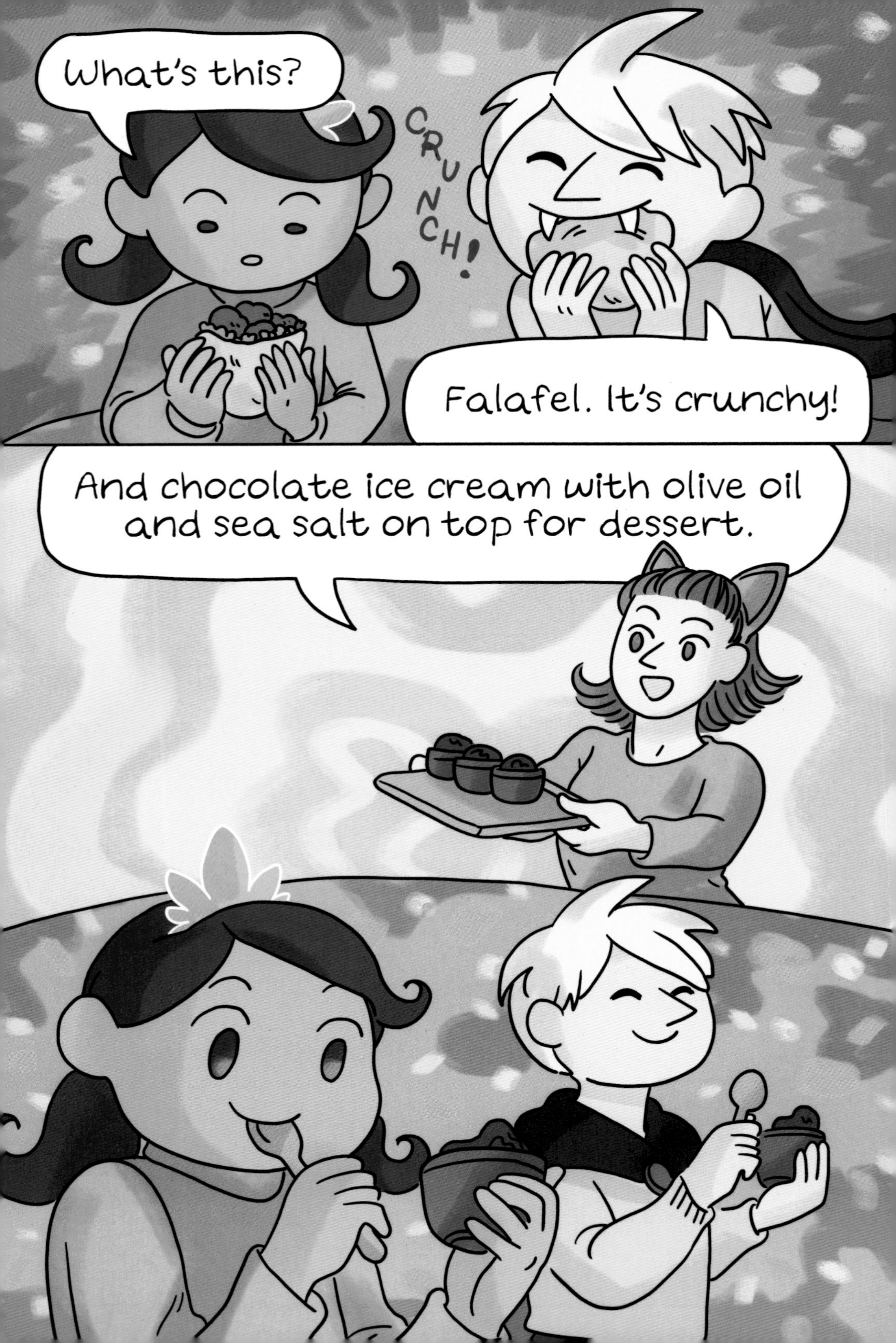
What's this?
CRUNCH!
Falafel. It's crunchy!
And chocolate ice cream with olive oil and sea salt on top for dessert.

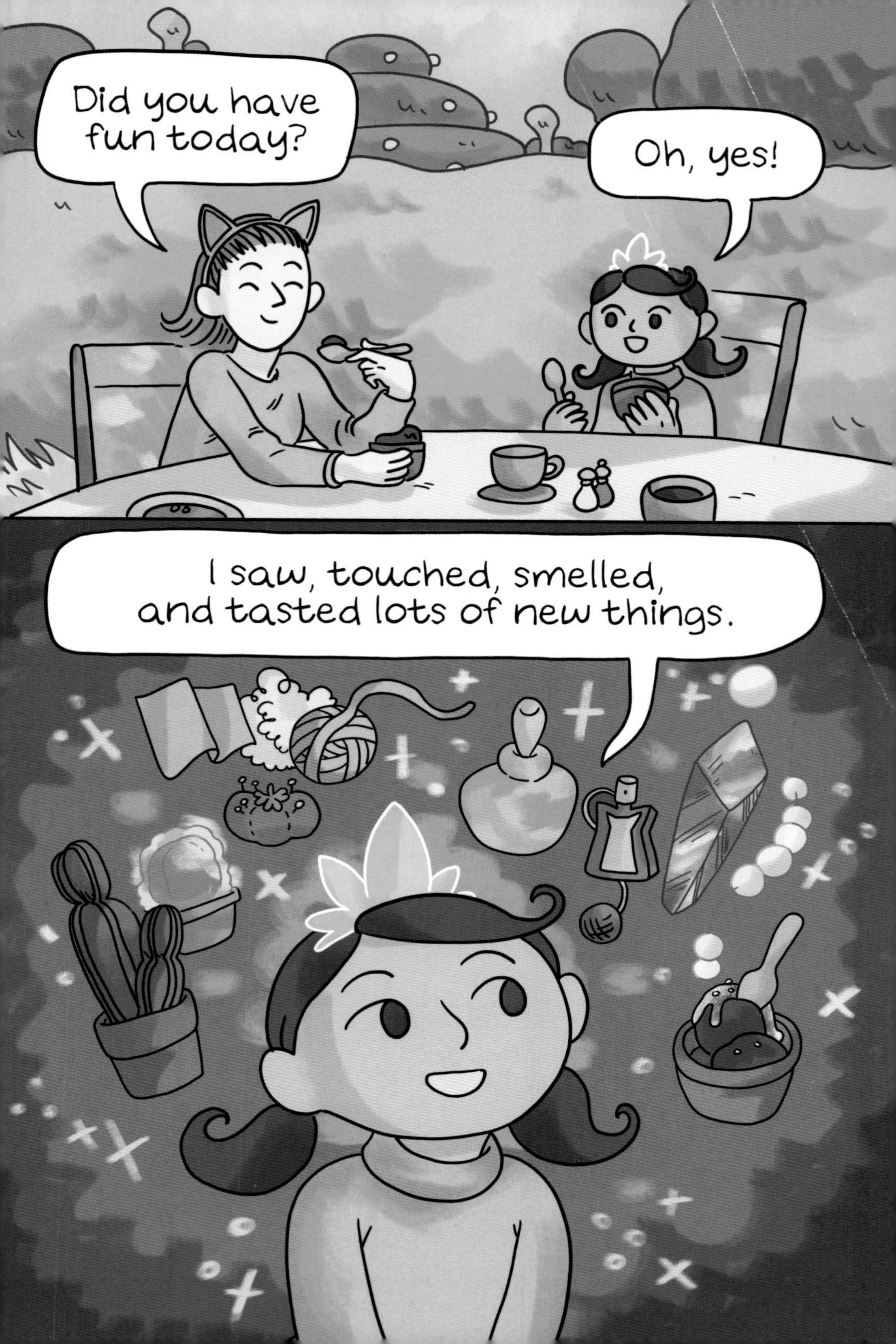
Did you have fun today?
Oh, yes!
I saw, touched, smelled, and tasted lots of new things.

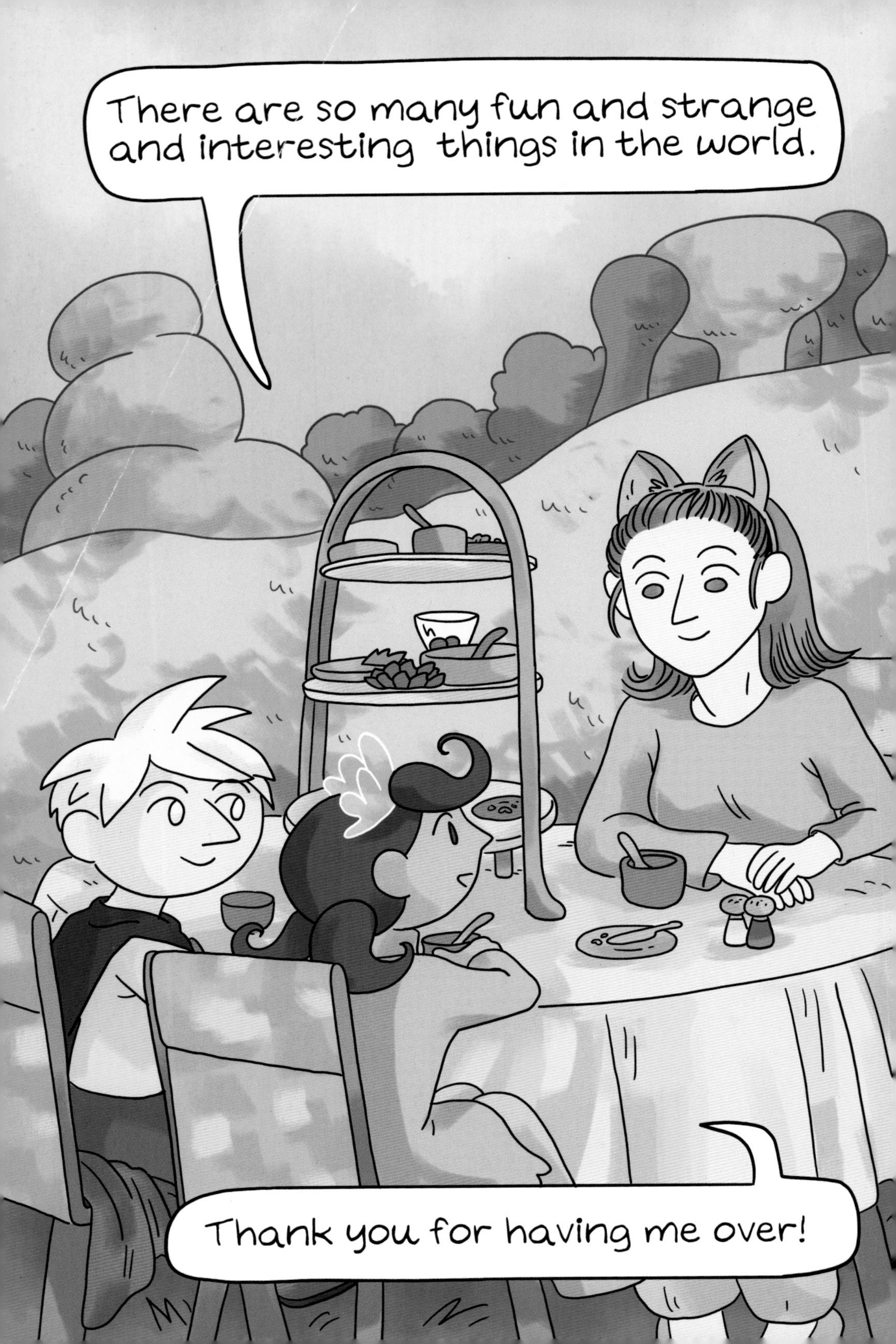
There are so many fun and strange and interesting things in the world.
Thank you for having me over!